MW01128324

Love Is a Breeze

Sarah Purcell

Published in the United States of America

Red Pen Warriors Publishing
Copyright 2015 Sarah Purcell
Cover design by Mike Grunsten and Kathryn Greiner
All rights reserved

ISBN – 13: 978-1480091139
ISBN – 10: 1480091138

All rights reserved. No part of this book may be reproduced or transmitted in any form or by any means, electronic or mechanical, including photocopying, recording, or by any information storage and retrieval system, without permission in writing, from the author.

This is a work of fiction. Names, characters, places and incidents, either are the product of the author's imagination or are used fictitiously. Any similarities to any persons, living or dead, places or evens are purely coincidental.

DEDICATION

I dedicate my first book to my family and friends who kept believing it was possible especially when I had my doubts. Thank you all for believing in me.

To my parents and grandparents who taught me I could do anything I put my mind to and to my brother, Tom, for instilling in me a love of words and reading. To my best friend, Shirley. I wish you could have read it. I miss you. May you all rest in peace.

When I first started writing romance, my aunt told me I should write something I know about, like a cookbook. Sorry, Aunt Frankie – what I know about cooking wouldn't fill a teaspoon!

Harriet – enjoy!

ACKNOWLEDGMENTS

A special thanks to my husband, Jim, my daughters, Kathy, Jane and Lyndi, my friends, Margaret and Jan for all their encouragement and pushing. Thanks to my friend, Cookie for her editing skills.

I also want to thank my friends at LERA for their support and encouragement. And, last but certainly not least my Red Pen Warriors – Jan, Helen, Shirley, Lee, Nancy, Robyn, Julia, Mike, Leslie and Tina. I could never have done it without you.

Table of Contents

CHAPTER ONE

Brianna Ryan had punched the down button for the elevator a third time when she heard her name called.

She turned around to see her best friend, Carly, running to catch up.

"What's your big hurry?" Carly asked.

Brianna heard the elevator door slide open and backed into it as she said, "I want to get home. I've made up my mind to break up with Eric. I want to get it over with."

"About time–" Carly froze, open-mouthed, her eyes wide.

Brianna knew of only one thing that caused that reaction in her usually animated friend. But it was too late. She collided with something– someone– solid. Strong hands steadied her as she stumbled over his feet. The doors closed with Carly still motionless on the other side.

"Perhaps you should try looking in the same direction as you are walking, Miss Ryan." The deep voice vibrated through her. She stepped to the side and turned to face him.

"I'm so sorry, Mr. Sharp. I was talking to my friend when the door opened."

"So I heard."

"Yes, well, I'm kind of in a hurry to get home. You see, I'm going to–"

"It's really none of my business, Miss Ryan."

Brianna felt the heat rise from her neck and settle on her cheeks. Facing forward, she clasped her hands in front of her and rocked back on her heels.

Awkward silence. Say something.

She glanced at him out of the corner of her eye. He stood with his arms crossed.

Looking anywhere but at the tall figure beside her, she took a deep breath and said, "Lovely weather we're having, isn't it?"

"Usually is at the end of April."

When the elevator stopped and the doors opened, he reached down and picked up his briefcase, moving closer to make room for two more passengers. Brianna chewed her thumbnail and released a nervous sigh.

"Relax, Miss Ryan." He looked down at her. "You'll be home soon enough."

She flicked her eyes his direction. "I know. It's just that—"

"Breaking up is hard to do?" He quirked an eyebrow. A smile played at the corner of his mouth.

Her mouth quivered when she attempted to smile. She licked her lips. "It truly isn't easy."

The elevator bumped to a stop on the ground floor. Mr. Sharp stood aside allowing the other passengers to exit. He followed Brianna into the lobby.

"I'm sure everything will work out. Good luck." He walked toward the parking garage entrance.

"Thank you." She said to his departing back.

He raised a hand in a parting salute before disappearing into the garage.

Brianna turned when she heard the second elevator door open. Carly rushed toward her.

"What happened?" She grabbed Brianna's arm.

"Nothing happened but it would have been a lot less awkward if you'd gotten on with me."

"I'm sorry, Bree, but you know the effect he has on me."

"Yeah, I do but he's just a man, Carly."

"That's like saying Everest is just a mountain or the Pacific is just some water, or the Mona Lisa is—"

"Just a painting." Brianna shook her head. "I get it."

"Don't tell me he doesn't have any effect on you. I know better."

"He's our boss. He makes me a little nervous but I don't turn into a statue every time he walks by." She opened the door and stepped into Chicago's pedestrian rush hour.

Carly followed. "I know he's our boss but he's also a gorgeous hunk of manhood."

"You're married." Brianna reminded her.

"Doesn't mean I can't enjoy the view." She nudged Brianna's shoulder. "You're not married and you'll soon be available."

"I've sworn off men, especially bossy ones, no matter how yummy they seem. It would be like jumping from the stove to the fireplace."

"You mean from the frying pan to the fire?" Carly laughed. "But fireplaces are romantic."

Brianna shook her head. "You're so full of blarney. You know that, right?"

"I just want you to be as happy as I am."

"I'll be very happy, ecstatic even, after tonight."

Looking up at the tall, athletic, blonde, Brianna cursed her shortness. If she had Carly's long legs she'd be home sooner. She could see over the throng of people and would feel the warmth of spring instead of the heat of bodies pressing all around her. She longed to burst free, see the new green leaves on the trees evenly spaced along the curb and smell the flowers at the corner cart. She released a nervous sigh.

"I don't know what to say. Words keep running through my head but I can't seem to get them in the right order."

"How about, 'It's over, jerk. Get out?' Short and simple. Works for me."

Brianna laughed. "I love you, Carly. You always say exactly what you think. But, I can't be mean, I don't want to hurt his feelings."

"Okay. He's leaving on that field trip thing tomorrow, right? Move out while he's gone and leave him a note. You'll have a month to find another place and get settled. He'll get the message and you won't have to hurt his feelings—if he even has any— not to his face, anyway."

"That's a coward's way out. I'm going to tell him tonight." She declared, then frowned. "Maybe I should wait until he gets back."

Carly punched Brianna's arm, hard. "Now that's the coward's way. Get it over with, Bree. You've put it off too long as it is."

Rubbing her shoulder, Brianna glared at Carly. "That hurt."

"Good. Now you're angry, and that's better than nice to deal with Eric."

"You're right, I know."

"Are you sure you don't want me to come with you? I don't trust that guy."

"Thanks but I'll be fine, really. I'll call you later."

They exchanged a brief hug before Carly turned to walk up her street.

Brianna watched her for a few seconds before continuing to her apartment. The pedestrian crowd thinned and she walked a little faster, her brightly colored skirt swished about her calves.

8

The temperature dropped with the sun as it moved lower behind the tall buildings. She wrapped her bulky sweater snuggly around her.

"Eric, this may not be the right time, but…No, too wishy-washy," she mouthed the words. "Eric, we both know things haven't been right for awhile– That's an understatement. Eric, we need to talk. To which he'll answer, 'Not now, Babe. I'm busy.'"

She hitched her oversized purse higher on her shoulder and raised her chin. Ascending the steps to her apartment building, she pressed the button and waited for Eric to buzz her in. Where is he? He's always home before me, she thought. She fished the key from the bottom of her bag and let herself in. Up one flight of stairs and down the hall she inserted the key into the lock of their apartment. She flipped the light switch on the wall and dropped her purse and keys onto the chest by the door.

She quickly scanned the room. Something was wrong.

"We've been robbed!" She clutched her throat and leaned against the door. The TV was gone, along with the DVD player and stereo. She willed her heart to be still and return to its place. The apartment was unusually quiet.

Strange. The DVR box and cable were still attached to the wall outlet. Another quick glance revealed some personal photos and books missing.

She ran to the bedroom. The TV, DVD player and clock radio in there were also missing. Returning to the living room, intent on calling the police, she glimpsed a note on the bathroom mirror. She walked toward the large yellow Post-it and pulled it from the glass.

Breeze,

    This may come as a shock to you, but I've decided this relationship is not working for me anymore. When I get back from my dig in Colombia, I'll be moving on. I hope you understand and will do the same. It's been fun, but it's over. I gave notice that I would not be renewing the lease so you'll have to be out by the end of the month.

              Eric

She reread the note before crumpling it into a tight ball and throwing it at the mirror.

"'The end of the month.' He decided! Who the bloody hell does he think he is? The jerk! Not working for him!" She kicked the toilet. The seat and lid dropped. She sat and rubbed her toe as Irish and English profanity swirled in her brain and exploded from her mouth.

She stood, stalked through the living room, grabbed her keys and headed for the superintendent's office on the ground floor. She danced from one foot to the other while she waited.

Finally, footsteps approached and she composed herself before the middle-aged woman opened the door. She was taller than Brianna, but who over the age of twelve wasn't. Brianna looked up to meet the super's questioning gaze.

"Hello, Mrs. Bergstrom. Did Eric pay the rent for May?" she asked.

"No, he didn't, Miss Ryan."

Damn!

"Okay. I'll give you a check in the morning."

"I'm afraid that won't work. He gave notice last month and said he'd be out by the end of April.

"That's this weekend! I thought he meant the end of next month. Could I extend it another month?"

"I'm afraid not. The apartment has been rented."

Crap!

"I do have a studio on the fourth floor that is available," Mrs. Bergstrom continued.

Brianna's eyes brightened.

"Perfect. I'll take it. Thank you." It's only a month earlier than she had planned to look for a place of her own. "I'll get a check."

"Tomorrow will be fine, Miss Ryan. Pity things didn't work out. Eric's such a charming man and those baby blue eyes." She waved a hand in front of her face as if she were experiencing a sudden hot flash.

Brianna's smile tightened.

Charming? Yeah, if you like snakes.

She turned and marched back upstairs. Crossing the room to the corner desk, she opened the top drawer. The checkbook wasn't there. Each drawer she opened she closed a little harder. They were all empty. She stormed into the bedroom, jerking and slamming each dresser drawer. Thankfully, her stuff was still there. Her third of the closet was untouched – she spread her wardrobe across the length of the rod. That's better, she thought with a slight smile.

In the bathroom her anger returned. Her make-up was there and her toothbrush, no toothpaste. How nice, he left her strawberry shampoo and conditioner. There was a damp towel slung on the shower rod. She opened the cabinet under the sink. Yep, he left the cleaning supplies and a couple of rolls of toilet paper. He took the hair dryer.

A search of the kitchen yielded one pan, dented and scratched. The coffee maker was gone but that was okay, she preferred tea. She opened another cabinet and breathed a sigh of relief. Her treasured teapot and Irish tea were there. No dishes, glasses or silverware. In the pantry she found a few paper plates, two plastic cups and half a box of plastic forks. He also had left all the food.

She reached for the cordless phone on the breakfast bar that divided the kitchen from the living room. Gone. She stomped to the plugged-in phone on the desk. Picking up the receiver, she listened for the dial tone. *Thank goodness he didn't have it shut off.* She wished she'd listened to Carly and gotten a cell phone but she saved everything she could for a place of her own and to continue art school.

Carrying the phone to the sofa, she was grateful for the furnished apartment, otherwise she'd be sitting and sleeping on the floor tonight.

As soon as Carly answered Brianna launched into a tirade. She had to hold the phone away from her ear while Carly strung together several colorful names.

"You can say whatever you like about Eric, just don't say, 'I told you so," Brianna said.

"I won't but you know I did."

Brianna leaned back on the couch, staring at the ceiling. "I know but it was nice being taken care of for a change."

"You allowed him way too much control. At least it's over and you didn't have to say anything." Carly concluded.

"You're right. All that worrying for nothing. There's a studio in this building I can have. I'm going to the bank first thing in the morning. I'll start moving after that. Not much to move, thanks to Eric.

* * * *

Early the next morning, Brianna showered and ate breakfast, anxious to get to the bank. Fresh start, day one.

She walked briskly, aided by a slight tailwind. She noticed the new green leaves and inhaled the

14

scent of the flowers. The warmth of the sun washed over her. By the time she reached the bank, she was practically singing *Oh, What a Beautiful Morning*. She flashed the security guard a brilliant smile and wished him a good morning. She crossed to the teller's window.

"Hi. I'm Brianna Ryan. I need to order some new checks and get some cash," she said, handing the teller her debit card.

"Certainly, Miss Ryan." The teller typed the account number into her computer. "This account was closed yesterday."

Brianna's smile faded.

"May I get cash from my savings account?"

"I'm afraid that has been closed, also."

"But that money was mine." Brianna's heart plummeted to her knees.

"I'm really sorry, Miss Ryan, but it was a joint account and Mr. Hanson was the primary holder."

Clutching her stomach, she willed her breakfast to stay put and walked to the nearest chair. *Now what?* She sank into the chair, attempting to sort through her jumbled thoughts. She recalled the day she told Eric she wanted to open a savings account and he said he could add her to his account. He never used the savings account. It made perfect sense at the time. She had struggled to keep food on the table and a roof over her and her aunt's heads since her uncle died when she was fifteen. Letting someone else handle the finances had been a great relief. Besides, the money saved on checks and account fees added to her savings. *How could I have been so stupid?* Opening her wallet, she counted her cash - four dollars and seventy-six cents.

If she were a crier now would be the time for it, but she wasn't. She brushed the hair from her face, stood and left the bank. Inside, her blood boiled. Bending her head into the wind, she marched back to the apartment. She stopped at the superintendant's office to let her know she wouldn't be able to rent the studio before going upstairs and calling Carly.

While waiting for her friend's arrival, she went to the small basement storage area. No surprise there – it was bare except for a couple of empty boxes. She took the cartons up to the apartment. As soon as she closed the door, the intercom buzzed.

"That was quick." She buzzed Carly in.

She opened the door and waited for Carly to ascend the stairs, which she did two at a time, carrying more empty boxes.

Carly was steaming and opened her mouth. Brianna raised her hand.

"You can't possibly say anything I haven't thought of. Let's just get on with it."

"I wish I could get my hands on the slime ball," Carly made a fist with one hand.

"No more than I do. You know he even took my paintings. What could he want those for? He hated my paintings. Said I was wasting my time and the smell of paint gave him a headache." Brianna put her hand to her mouth and gasped. "I just realized he took my laptop. The weasel. He had no right to take that."

"Maybe you should call the police." Carly suggested.

"He's in Colombia by now. I'll deal with him when he gets back. This is why I've sworn off men. I'll never trust one again."

"Never's a long time, Bree. There are some good men out there. Look at Rob. He's great."

"You've only been married a month, Carly. You're still on your honeymoon." Brianna said. "Are you sure it's okay with him that I stay with you?"

"Sure, he's fine with it. I told you he's a good man," She grabbed a box. "I'll pack the kitchen and living room. You do the bathroom and bedroom. We'll be out of here in no time."

An hour later Carly stowed the last box in the back of her ancient Honda hatchback and slammed the door.

"I'm starved," she said as she slid behind the wheel. "Let's stop for a burger. My treat."

"I guess it will have to be. I have less than five dollars until next payday. That's two weeks."

"I told you I can lend you a few bucks 'til then."

"And I told you, I'll not be borrowing money from you. Thanks for the offer though but I'll be fine. It's enough that you're letting me stay with you."

"The offer stands. First thing Monday morning remember to stop the direct deposit on your paycheck."

"I will." Brianna nodded as Carly drove up to the drive-thru window of the nearest fast-food restaurant.

CHAPTER TWO

Brianna rolled onto her stomach nearly toppling off the air mattress wedged between the dining table and the wall. She pulled the pillow over her head to muffle the whispers coming from the sofa bed. She dozed fitfully until a light in the kitchen area filled the room. She turned to face the wall, pulling the pillow tighter over her head. It was no use. Kicking off the covers, she sat up and yawned. She raked her fingers through her hair. Even the sun was still asleep.

"Morning," she said when she saw Rob standing by the sink eating from a bowl.

"Sorry, I tried to be quiet. I'm scheduled for an early shift today." Rob was an intern at a nearby hospital.

"It's okay. I couldn't sleep anyway. Too much on my mind, I guess." Brianna stood, stretched the kinks out of her back and padded barefoot to the bathroom.

When she returned, Rob was dressed in blue scrubs and heading for the door.

"See you later. Don't worry about waking Carly. She'd sleep through a tornado."

"Have a good day. And, thanks again, Rob."

"No problem." He smiled as he closed the door behind him.

Brianna opened the cupboard and pulled out the box of Froot Loops she'd brought and poured some into a bowl. The sound echoed in the tiny space. She glanced at Carly still sleeping like the dead. Carefully easing the refrigerator door open, she grabbed her carton of milk and emptied it into the bowl. She sat at the table, facing the window and looked at the city lights twinkling like stars.

This is not going to work. She looked around. Besides a bathroom and a large closet, this was it – one room.

While she microwaved water for tea she heard a thud and opened the door to find the newspaper lying on the floor. She retrieved it and sat at the table, stirring her tea while she looked at

20

available rentals. Not that she could do anything right now but it wouldn't hurt to look. By the time she finished the classifieds and the comics, the sun peeked around the tall buildings and Carly struggled to rejoin the living.

"Rob leave already?" She asked, propping herself on one elbow.

"Yeah, about two hours ago."

"What time is it?"

"Seven."

Carly groaned and flopped back onto her pillow.

"Is there any coffee?" Carly sat up, swung her feet to the floor and shook her short blonde hair into place.

"No. Rob said he'd get some at the hospital. I think he just didn't want to wake me. I can make some now, if you'd like."

"That'd be great," Carly replied before heading to the bathroom.

Brianna filled the coffee maker and set it to brew while she reheated her tea. She carried her cup to the table and sat. Carly joined her with her mug.

"How'd you sleep?" Carly asked, adding cream and sugar to her coffee.

21

"Pretty good," Brianna blushed slightly, remembering the quiet giggles coming from the bathroom during the newlyweds' late shower.

"Liar," Carly said. "You have circles under your eyes. If I didn't know better, I'd think you had a hangover."

Brianna smiled, "Well, you know, strange place, strange noises."

"Right." Carly grinned.

"I looked at the rental ads. There doesn't seem to be much available in my price range."

"There will be in a couple of weeks. This is the first of the month."

"I hope so."

"What? You don't like my palace?"

"I love your 'palace,' Carly. You and Rob are like family. You are the closest to family I have in the States, but 'three's a crowd,' as they say. Lord knows I'm used to a crowd, growing up with four brothers in a small farm house and only one bathroom but you guys need your privacy."

"That must have been fun. Rob has one sister and I'm an only child."

Brianna's eyes clouded with memories. "Sometimes it was but the boys were quite a bit older and bossed me around terribly.

"That makes it even more of a mystery why you hooked up with Eric. He was such a control freak."

"He wasn't at first. I guess I was at a vulnerable place in my life. My aunt, who I lived with since I was fourteen, had just died. We'd been dating for a couple of years. I thought I knew him and I trusted him. We'd even talked about marriage. When he asked me to move in with him it seemed like the perfect solution."

"I think you're lucky." Carly took a sip of her coffee.

"Lucky? I don't feel very lucky right now."

"Men with control issues often turn violent."

"Oh, I don't think Eric's a violent person." Brianna leaned back in her chair. "Though he did have a bit of a temper. I thought he might hit me when I told him I'd signed up for an art class. He was furious."

"You're amazing, Bree. I'd probably be bitter as hell."

"Life's too short to waste on sour apples." She stood and cleared the table. "Enough maudlin talk. I'll wash up."

"After I make up the bed, let's vegg-out and watch movies all day. Tomorrow, it's back to work."

"Sounds good to me," Brianna said. "No sappy love stories, though. I'm in the mood for murder and mayhem."

"You got it." Carly laughed.

* * * *

After another restless night Brianna rose early, intending to take a shower before anyone else woke up. Rob had the day off and was trying to catch up on his sleep. He had a pillow pulled tightly over his head. Carly was already in the shower. She reversed direction and tip-toed to the kitchen. As quietly as possible she made a cup of tea and spread cream cheese on a bagel.

"All yours," Carly called in a loud whisper before ducking into the closet to get dressed.

"Thanks." She sat at the little table to eat. When she finished, she squeezed by the sofa-bed and into the bathroom.

Refreshed by the warm shower, she wiped the steam off the mirror and combed out her wavy hair. She plugged in the hair dryer then unplugged it, afraid the noise would wake Rob. She pulled her hair into a damp pony tail instead.

Carly knocked on the door. "I need my make-up."

"All done," she said as she opened the door and went into the closet to dress. She put her make-up in her purse to put on at work.

* * * *

Carly and Brianna were the last bodies to squeeze into the crowded elevator ascending to the twenty-ninth floor where they worked at Sharp Advertising, the top ad agency in Chicago.

Brianna left Carly in the employees' lounge fixing a cup of coffee and eating a muffin from the vending machine. She went into the ladies' room where she put on her make-up and adjusted her pony-tail. Coming out of the restroom she met Carly, who was brushing crumbs off her shirt. They walked together to the weekly department meeting.

Their supervisor, Miss Davis, stood at the front of the room, pushed her round, black-rimmed glasses up her nose as she pursed her thin lips and counted heads arriving for the meeting. Eccentric but an amazing graphic artist, she resembled a pencil with a straight brown bob on top, wrapped in a short, red pleated skirt and black shirt, both salvaged from the seventies.

The warm   stale air of the windowless room and lack of sleep, caused Brianna to nod off. Carly jabbed her with an elbow. This was going to be a very long day. She sat up straight and tried to follow Miss Davis' animated speech as she swooped back and forth across the room.

"Mr. Sharp will be out of town this week but we still have work to do," Miss Davis concluded and dismissed her underlings.

A plan instantly formed in Brianna's mind. She pulled Carly aside and whispered in her ear.

"What? Are you out of your mind?" Carly stepped back and stared at her.

"Shhh," Brianna put her finger to her lips and looked around. Everyone else made their way to their cubicles and, other than a glance from a couple of girls, no one paid any attention to them.

"Mr. Sharp is out of town, though it wouldn't matter - you could set a watch by his coming and going. I wouldn't be bothering anybody and it'd only be until payday. It's perfect."

"It is not 'perfect.' It's insane." Carly retorted.

"I'll sleep on the sofa in the lounge. You can bring me food and clothes."

Carly grabbed Brianna by the shoulders, turning her and bending so they were nose to nose.

"Bree, are you listening to me? This could get us both fired."

"No, it won't. I won't involve you."

"I'm already involved."

Brianna leaned her forehead on Carly's. "You're a great friend, Carly. I'll go home with you tonight, pack a few things and tomorrow I'll move in here." She turned and practically skipped to her desk.

Carly shook her head. Once Bree made up her mind there was no stopping her.

CHAPTER THREE

John Sharp unlocked the doors to his ten-year old Chicago advertising agency, thinking the day couldn't possibly get any worse. After a weeklong business trip to Phoenix, his flight home the day before sat on the runway for two and a half hours in the relentless Arizona heat. This morning his coffee maker malfunctioned and spewed brown gunk all over his kitchen and his routine morning workout at his condo's gym didn't happen because of a broken water pipe. When the elevator in his office building inexplicably stopped at the twenty-first floor and refused to go any further, he walked the remaining eight floors to his office after working out in the first floor gym. He was surprised to find his private office door locked. Slipping his key into the lock, he pushed open the door. Singing came from the adjoining bathroom.

Great. I'm dripping in sweat and the cleaning crew is still here. I need a shower and a strong cup of coffee. John didn't like it when things disrupted his schedule.

He reached for the bathroom knob but paused when he heard the shower running and a female voice singing a bawdy Irish ditty. The cleaning crew isn't Irish. He leaned against the opposite wall with arms folded across this chest, ankles crossed and waited.

* * * *

Brianna rinsed the shampoo from her hair and turned off the shower. She stepped out of the tiled enclosure, grabbed a towel from the stack on the shelf and quickly dried. Wrapping the towel around herself, she reached for another and opened the door. Bending over to secure the second towel around her head, she stepped into the narrow hallway. She collided with something. Her body froze. Her heart fell somewhere around her knees. This could not be good. She opened her eyes and slowly raised her head taking in the long legs, narrow hips, flat stomach, well-muscled chest beneath a Nike t-shirt and strong jaw before encountering the piercing gray eyes of her boss.

"I see you don't do much better walking forward, Miss Ryan."

She stared, dumbfounded, for a few seconds before her tongue bypassed her brain. "What are you doing here at this hour? You never come in before eight o'clock or after eight for that matter, always eight on the dot. Never—" She looked at her bare wrist.

"—seven," he said, glancing at his watch. "I came in early to work out here because my gym was closed." The deep, male voice sent shivers down her spine. "Why am I explaining anything to you? You're the trespasser. Why are you here, in my office, in a towel?" His eyes sparked.

She backed toward the leather sofa, "My clothes are on the sofa," she said, as if that explained everything.

Brianna stood still as she watched his eyes travel from her turbaned head to her vivid purple toenails. Fingers of warmth spread wherever his eyes lingered.

She crossed her arms over her chest partly to control the trembling that threatened to overtake her, mostly to keep the towel from slipping. "May I get dressed now? It's rather cold in here," she said. His right eyebrow shot up but, otherwise he didn't move.

"Get dressed in the bathroom and be quick about it. I can't deal with a girl in a towel."

"It's steamy in there."

30

He pinned her with a warning glare. "You have exactly five minutes," he said, before walking out of the room.

John passed his secretary's vacant desk and looked out the window at tiny cars rushing about on Michigan Avenue. The sun cast a golden trail as it rose across the rippling surface of Lake Michigan. He rubbed the back of his neck. His brain told him he should fire her but his heart, which normally wasn't involved in business matters, said otherwise. Something about the girl intrigued him. There was a vulnerability about her despite her bravado. There was a whole lot of woman packed into that little body. He took a deep breath. Her scent reminded him of the strawberry shortcake his grandmother used to make. Her hair was even the color of strawberries – no, more like sun-dried tomatoes, mounds of wavy, sun-dried tomatoes falling on creamy white... Swiping his hand down his face, he shook his head, an effort to stop thinking like a hormone crazed teenager. Fortunately, no one would be here for another hour. He wanted to resolve this before any other employees arrived.

John turned as a tall, elegant blonde, one of his ad executives, entered the reception area.

"This is taking Casual Friday to a whole new level." She looked him up and down. "John, I—"

His private office door swung open and Brianna poked her head out. "You can come back in now," she said.

He looked from one to the other. *Damn.* "I don't have time to talk to you right now, Kaitlyn,"

The blonde's ice blue eyes narrowed as she looked from one to the other before turning on her heel and stalking down the hall.

John turned back to the girl in his office. He brushed past her and stood beside his massive teak desk.

She tugged at the hem of her short skirt and fidgeted with the neck of her green cotton sweater. Simple flat shoes hid her purple nail polish.

Brianna smoothed her hair and squirmed under his scrutiny. He blinked.

"Please, be seated." He indicated one of the leather chairs in front of his desk. The scent of strawberries hung in the air as she passed him and sat in the specified chair. He inhaled sharply and leaned against the corner of his desk, arms braced on either side of him.

"I hope you have a good explanation for this."

"I usually take a shower at night but I lost track of time and was so tired I decided to get up early and do it. Anyway, you're supposed to be in Phoenix." He said 'start talking' not 'engage brain.'

He looked at her. Her emerald green eyes never wavered from his. He liked that.

"Why were you taking a shower in my office at all?"

"It's the only one on this floor," she offered and noticed his eyes narrow and darken.

"Would you mind sitting down? I'm getting a kink in my neck looking up at you." Brianna rubbed the back of her neck. From her vantage point he looked about seven feet tall but, since her nose had been level with his breastbone, he was, in reality, a little over a foot taller than her five-foot two. Six foot-three or four, solid muscle, long legs, great body… She reined in her thoughts when she met his piercing gray eyes.

Their eyes locked for a second before John turned away. "I'd like the whole story before the rest of the employees show up and I'm in no mood for games or lies." He moved around the desk and sat in the large leather chair. Picking up a pencil, he tapped it on the blotter.

Her hand went to her head as she attempted to smooth the unruly mass of curls and wished for something to keep it out of her face.

"You can call me Bree, that's what my friends and my mum call me. Or Breeze, that's what my dad calls me. I won't go into what my brothers call me. And, I don't lie." She raised her head a notch.

"Breeze?" He put up his hand. "Never mind, I don't want to know. I do want to know exactly why you were taking a shower here, anywhere, in this building. Is there no shower where you live, Miss Ryan?"

"Well, you see, there's the problem. I don't have a place to live at the moment."

"Are you telling me you're living here?" His tone rose half an octave, warning Brianna that his patience was wearing thin.

Brianna took a deep, calming breath. *Lord, control my tongue.*

"I had to move out of my apartment last weekend. I have no money and nowhere to go, so, I've been sleeping on the sofa in the employee's lounge." She glanced up and gave him a small smile. "My parents still live in Ireland. Obviously, I can't run to them. Not that I would because I'm an adult and can take care of myself."

He raised an eyebrow. "I take it the break-up did not go well."

"Not exactly as planned, no." She went on, "The girls I know all live in small apartments with two or three roommates and besides, I wouldn't want to intrude on them so here I am, not bothering anybody — until today, that is. " She gave him another tiny smile. "Anyway..."

John listened as the Irish lilt of her voice became more pronounced. He focused on the movement of her full lips and the way freckles danced on her upturned nose and spilled across her cheekbones. His eyes dropped lower when she paused for a deep breath before going on with her explanation. He raised his eyes back to hers.

"... Really, you wouldn't even have known I was here if you'd kept to your routine."

He realized she had stopped talking when she finally took another breath and licked her upper lip.

"Is there really no one you could stay with?"

"I stayed with Carly and her new husband for the weekend but they only have a studio and it was — awkward." She glanced at him.

"Yes, I can see how that would be an uncomfortable situation but—"

Brianna turned away from his gaze and studied the painting on the wall. She forced her eyes back to him. "May I go now? I have a lot of work to do."

"Just like that, you have 'work to do.' Doesn't any of this seem odd to you?"

"Well, yes. I admit it's a wee bit odd."

He laughed out loud, a deep rich sound. "A wee bit?"

Warmth rushed to her cheeks. "Okay, a lot odd, but I really had no choice." Her gaze fell to her hands folded in her lap.

"There are always choices, Miss Ryan."

"Ah, yes. I had so many choices." She raised her head and looked directly into his eyes. "It's warmer and safer here than on a park bench, cleaner and quieter than the bus depot and it has a shower." In one fluid movement she rose, turned on her heel and walked out of his office.

"Why can't I learn to think before I speak," Brianna scolded herself. If anyone offered lessons in tongue control she vowed to be first in line. She made her way to the employees lounge on shaky legs. Carly, thankfully, was alone.

Collapsing onto the sofa, she rested her head on the arm and covered her eyes with her forearm.

"You will not believe what just happened."

"What?" Carly looked at Bree's reflection in the mirror. She stopped, mascara wand in midair and turned. "Oh, no! You got caught, didn't you?"

Brianna nodded beneath her arm.

"The cleaning crew?" Carly asked.

Brianna shook her head. She'd managed to avoid the cleaning crew, which wasn't that difficult. They had iPods stuck in their ears and bopped around with their eyes closed.

"Miss Davis?"

Brianna sat up. "Mr. Sharp."

Carly's jaw dropped, her blue eyes widened. "Oh. My. God! Come on, out with it. What did he say? Did he fire you? I've heard he can be fair. Of course, I've also heard he can be hard as granite. They don't call him Sharp the Shark for nothing, you know. How'd he catch you?"

"I sort of bumped into him as I came out of his bathroom."

Carly sat down next to her while Brianna told her the details. Carly buried her face in her hands but her shaking shoulders gave away her uncontrolled laughter.

"It's not funny, Carly. I'm probably going to lose my job. That's just what I need right now.

Eric takes off with all my money and I lose my job."

"I'm surprised the shark didn't fire you on the spot," Carly said, wiping her eyes with the back of her hand.

"I didn't give him a chance. I had to make a hasty exit before I threw up all over his big, shiny desk."

Carly flung a comforting arm across Bree's shoulders as they left the lounge and walked to their cubicles.

"Not a word of this to anyone. Promise?"

Carly gave her an evil grin.

"Carly!" Brianna warned.

"Oh, okay. But I have to tell Rob."

She might as well get some work done while waiting for the ax to fall. She hated losing this job. It fulfilled her creative spirit and paid the rent, or would if she had rent to pay.

She worked on drawings for an ad campaign for the Illinois Wildlife Preserve, a project she poured her heart into. Painting nature scenes was her true passion.

She didn't realize how much time had passed until Carly peered over the wall separating their cubicles. "Come on. I'll buy you lunch. You need a change of scenery."

"That I do!" Brianna said, although she was certain her scenery was going to change soon anyway.

"Emily and Liv are coming, too"

"Fine. But not a word about this to them," Brianna repeated her warning. Emily and Liv were co-captains of the inter-departmental gossip team, one might even consider them gold medalists.

Preferring to concentrate on eating, Brianna remained quiet during lunch. She hadn't had time to eat the muffin Carly brought her for breakfast. No one noticed her silence because Emily and Liv were eagerly filling them in on all the latest gossip. Brianna barely listened until the name "Kaitlyn" caught her attention.

"I think they're perfect for each other," Liv said. "He's a shark and she's a shark hunter."

"Who?" Brianna asked.

"Kaitlyn Schuster and the boss," Emily said.

"Is she a tall blonde?" Brianna asked.

"Yeah, the Arctic Queen. Why?

"Oh, nothing. I saw her this morning and wondered who she was. I've seen her before, just never knew her name. She and the boss are a couple?"

"She wishes," Liv said. "She knows the fastest way up the corporate ladder."

"Personally, I think she's a cold bitch." Carly said.

"I think they are perfect for each other. They're both cold-blooded creatures," said Emily.

"I think he's hot!" Liv said. "Too bad he's so aloof."

* * * *

Miss Davis stood by the elevator when the doors opened.

"Mr. Sharp wants to see you in his office," she said, eyeing her over the top of her black-rimmed glasses.

She exchanged a quick glance with Carly, ignored the wide-eyed stares of Emily and Liv and said to her supervisor, "When?"

"Now."

"Good luck," Carly whispered, giving her a quick hug before walking down the hall to the graphics department. Brianna watched her go.

"Now! Miss Ryan."

"Yes, ma'am." Brianna walked off in the opposite direction toward the executive suites. She looked down at the plush green carpet. How fitting. The Green Mile. Executed, terminated, same thing.

She squared her shoulders and raised her head. She may go down but she'd go with dignity. She walked past the reception desk to Mr. Sharp's secretary and announced, "I'm Brianna Ryan. Mr. Sharp is expecting me."

"Yes, Miss Ryan." She led Brianna to his office door, knocked lightly and opened it.

"Miss Ryan is here, sir."

"Show her in." His deep voice carried through the crack in the door. The secretary smiled as she stepped aside.

Mr. Sharp stood and stepped around his desk when Brianna entered the room. She stood with her trembling hands clutched behind her back, focusing her gaze on the perfect knot of his red tie. He'd been less intimidating in his workout clothes.

"Please sit down," he said, indicating one of the leather chairs in front of his desk.

"If you're going to fire me, I'd prefer to stand, thank you."

His eyes narrowed as he studied her face. "The thought did cross my mind but I'm not going to fire you—yet." He pointed at the chair again.

Brianna perched on the edge of the chair, clasping her still shaking hands in her lap. He returned to his chair behind the wide desk. Picking up a pencil, he idly tapped it on the shiny teak surface, thumbing through a stack of papers. For several minutes he shuffled the papers while uttering, "Hmms," and "Ahhs.

Brianna shifted in her chair and cast a quick glance at the wall clock. Only three minutes had passed. It seemed like an hour.

She leaned back in the chair, sat up again and cleared her throat. "Since you're not going to fire me – yet." She tilted her head, offering a slight smile. "I'd like to go back to work. I have a deadline to meet." She placed her hands on the arms of the chair in preparation to stand.

"Excuse me?" He looked up.

"I said, 'I'd like to…'"

"I heard what you said, Miss Ryan. Apparently, patience isn't one of your virtues."

Brianna thought she detected a slight smile and an amused twinkle in his eyes.

"No, sir. I find it difficult to sit still for long. That's one of the reasons my dad calls me Breeze.

I'm always moving but I get the job done. And, I really do have a lot of work to do. Sir."

"Relax, Miss Ryan." Mr. Sharp smiled again.

Holy Cow! She sucked in air and leaned back in the chair.

He cocked an eyebrow. "I've been looking over your work records. Except for the fact that you're living here, you are the model employee. Never late or sick, always meet deadlines and your artwork is quite remarkable. While your dedication to your work is commendable you simply cannot live here. Have you been able to come up with an alternative?

"It would only be another week, until pay day. I'll stay out of your shower. You won't even know I'm here."

"Believe me, I'd know you were here. This is not about the shower, Miss Ryan. You cannot stay here and that's final. I suggest you spend the remainder of the afternoon making other arrangements."

Frustration bubbled inside her and released the wayward tongue she had tried so hard to control.

"What is it that you don't understand about the fact that I don't have any money? None. Zip. I know that's hard for you to imagine." She looked around the richly decorated office. *Are you trying to get yourself fired?* "I'm not complaining, I just need time, one week, until payday."

His gray eyes locked with her green ones for several seconds before he reached for the phone.

"I'll arrange for an advance on your pay so you'll be able to find something suitable."

Could her luck possibly be changing? Relief coursed through her and she relaxed into the chair.

Interrupted by a knock on the door, he looked up as Kaitlyn Schuster walked in. He stood as she approached the desk. She cast a glacial frown at Brianna before turning to Mr. Sharp with a seductive smile. Bree shivered, certain the temperature dropped several degrees. She studied the back of the statuesque platinum blonde clad in a dove-gray dress. Probably Valentino, she thought.

"John, don't forget we have a meeting with the Henderson group tomorrow night at seven. Why don't you pick me up and we'll go together?"

"I haven't forgotten, Kaitlyn. I'll pick you up at 6:30. It's at the Drake, right?"

"Make it 6:00 and we can have a drink before the meeting." She gave Brianna another icy glance before she turned on her designer stilettos and marched out of the room, leaving a trail of Obsession in her wake. Brianna wrinkled her nose and sneezed.

"I don't think she was happy to see me here," Brianna said, wiping her hand on her skirt.

Mr. Sharp furrowed an eyebrow as he reached for the phone again. "I'll have Mrs. Wilson call you when your check is ready. In the meantime, make some phone calls and find more suitable accommodations."

"Yes, sir and thank you. You've been very kind." She stood up.

"Not all sharks are killers, Miss Ryan." He smiled again. Brianna grasped the back of the chair willing her knees not to buckle.

She countered with a puny smile of her own and walked stiffly out of the room.

* * * *

At five o'clock, Brianna stood at the elevators chatting with her co-workers when the hairs on the back of her neck stood up. A hand at her elbow turned her insides to Jello. The chitchat stopped, eyes rounded and jaws dropped. She turned and met a pair of steel gray eyes.

"Miss Ryan. May I have a word with you?"

"You go on, I'll call you later," she said to the Carly statue as the elevator doors opened.

45

She turned and followed Mr. Sharp to an area away from the bank of elevators, already dreading the barrage of questions she'd face Monday from the gossip team.

"Were you able to find a place to stay?"

"Yes, I found a room that will do temporarily until I can afford an apartment. I cashed the check so I'm all set. Thank you." She smiled brightly.

"You're welcome." He returned the smile.

Another elevator door opened and they both turned. His light touch on Brianna's back sent a current up her spine. They stepped into the car and the door closed. Mr. Sharp greeted a few people already in the elevator. She was in a small space with the most devastatingly handsome man she had ever seen. They stopped a couple of floors down and several more people crowded into the small car, jostling her closer to him. She had trouble breathing and her heart raced like a marathon runner. Her palms were sweaty. He's my boss, she kept reminding herself. Finally, the elevator reached the ground floor. They stepped out.

"See you Monday." Brianna gave a little wave and headed for the entrance.

Mr. Sharp turned toward the entry to the parking garage, stopped and turned back. He pulled a business card from his pocket and wrote on the back.

"This is my cell number in case you need anything." He handed her the card. "Do you need a ride?"

She dropped the card into her purse. "Oh. No. I'll take the bus but thank you for the offer."

Brianna watched as he disappeared through the door before slinging her bulging backpack over one shoulder and walking to the corner bus stop.

CHAPTER FOUR

John looked up when the door opened and a cool breeze rushed into Jake's Bar and Grill. A hush fell over the patrons seated at the bar. Heads turned and followed the stunning blonde as she sashayed across the room. He shook his head and sipped his scotch on the rocks. Wishing he'd taken the seat not facing the door, or even better, was invisible, he swirled the glass one way then the other. He seemed fascinated by the movement of the liquid against the cubes. He looked up again when the woman slid onto the bench across from him.

"I think you are the only man in this room who didn't notice me," she said.

"You're hard to ignore, Kaitlyn."

"And, yet, you do it so easily."

"What brings you here?" John asked with a slight smile.

"You. And, I must say, you don't seem very happy to see me," Kaitlyn said, jutting her bright red, bottom lip into a pout.

"Just surprised. This place isn't up to your usual standards." John finished his drink and signaled the cocktail waitress.

"I felt like seafood and this is one of the best. Besides, I knew it was your favorite and took a chance you'd be here."

John raised an eyebrow. "What is so pressing it couldn't wait until tomorrow night?"

The waitress set another scotch if front of John, picked up the empty glass and turned to Kaitlyn.

"What would you like, ma'am?"

"Vodka martini, very dry. Gray Goose, if you have it. And, I want it with two olives, not onions," Kaitlyn said.

"Thank you, Liz." John smiled at the waitress.

"Can't I have a drink with a friend?" Kaitlyn looked through her lashes.

"Of course, but you said you were looking for me. There must be a reason."

The waitress set Kaitlyn's drink in front of her and turned to John, "Your table is ready, sir."

He stood and turned to Kaitlyn. "Would you care to join me for dinner?"

"I'd love to." Kaitlyn slid out of the booth and hooked her arm through his, licking her lips like a kitten savoring the cream. They followed the waitress to a small table in the dining room. John held a chair for Kaitlyn before seating himself.

"Your waitress will be with you shortly," Liz said, handing them menus.

Kaitlyn perused the menu a moment.

"Who was that redhead in your office this morning?" she said without looking up.

Ah, the real reason for the visit. "One of the graphic artists."

"Oh? Her work is not up to standards? Doesn't Human Resources usually deal with employee issues?"

"It was personal, not an HR problem. And, quite the contrary, her work is very good. Exceptional, actually."

Kaitlyn looked up, raising one perfectly penciled brow.

"Oh. Since when do you handle employees' personal problems?"

"It really isn't your concern, Kaitlyn. Let's order, shall we?" He signaled the waitress.

Kaitlyn frowned and narrowed her eyes.

"I haven't decided yet." She looked down at the menu, turning the pages back and forth. "I came into work early this morning because I wanted to talk to you about something but you were clearly preoccupied with that girl."

"You had all day to speak with me. Now you've gone out of your way to find me. What is so urgent, Kaitlyn?"

Kaitlyn glared at John. "I tried twice. Both times *she* was there." She lowered her lashes and formed her lips into a seductive pout. "I heard Charlie Myers is retiring soon. I want his position."

"He may be," John said. "I'll consider you when the time comes."

The waitress approached the table and addressed Kaitlyn.

"I want the spinach salad, raspberry vinaigrette on the side and no onions, broiled sea scallops with drawn butter, no garlic. Steamed, fresh vegetables instead of potatoes. And another one of these." She pushed her martini glass toward the waitress.

The waitress nodded, took the glass and turned to John.

"I'll have the fillet, rare. Baked potato, loaded and the Cesar salad, please." He smiled at her. "You're new, aren't you? What's your name?"

"Maya. I started last week." She returned his smile. "Would you care for another drink, also?"

"No, I'll have coffee, black. Thanks, Maya."

Kaitlyn raised both perfect eyebrows and looked at John with a hint of green in her ice blue eyes.

"Flirting with the help, are we?"

"I was simply being polite, Kaitlyn."

"Your politeness will have her drooling all over my dinner." Kaitlyn huffed.

John gave a slight shake of his head but said nothing.

"I have some concerns about our meeting with the Henderson Group tomorrow night. I think—"

John held up a hand in protest. "No work talk. I'm sure you have everything under control, as usual."

Maya brought their food. John relished every mouthful while Kaitlyn picked at her meal, clearly piqued at John's lack of interest.

"Would you like dessert?" Maya asked while clearing the plates.

John looked at Kaitlyn. She shook her head.

"No, thank you," he said, ignoring Kaitlyn's miffed grumble. "I would like another cup of coffee." He smiled. Kaitlyn simmered.

When they rose to leave, Kaitlyn swayed slightly and placed a hand on John's chest to steady herself.

"Ooh, I feel a little tipsy," she said, looking up through her thickly mascaraed lashes. "Perhaps you should drive me home."

"Since when do you get tipsy on two martinis?" he said, recognizing her ploy and removing her hand from his jacket. "I'll get you a cab."

Kaitlyn straightened, cast him a cold look and said, "I'll drive myself." She strode to the door without looking back.

John shook his head, put down a generous tip and left the restaurant.

* * * *

Brianna sat on the edge of the sagging bed, hands covering her ears and cursing the strong Irish frugality that led her to this seedy residence hotel. It seemed like a good idea at the time. She wanted to save money for a real apartment and the pictures on the website didn't look bad. Now, she was surprised they even had a website. *The Washington Plaza*. She smirked, a grand-sounding name for such a dump but it was near the bus stop and only a twenty minute ride to work but how was she going to work if she couldn't get any sleep?

Outside the door of her grungy room a couple of men argued in loud, slurring voices. In the street below her grimy window cars screeched and backfired, sirens blared continuously. The bed squeaked as she collapsed onto it, wrapping the hard pillow around her ears. It was no use, the sounds penetrated and the stench of the pillow made her eyes water and stomach churn.

She got up and walked to the window, pulled back the dusty, tattered curtain and peered over the rusty metal fire escape. The street was lit up like the Vegas strip, neon signs blinking the names of various businesses: *Girls, Girls, Girls!* blinked one, *oe's Place* blinked another—the *J* was dead, probably hit by a stray bullet. Sly's Swap 'n' Shop was closed and secured with pull-down steel gates, but *Candi's Adult Video* with its flashing marquee was doing a brisk business.

Brianna dropped the curtain and returned to the bed. Tomorrow she would buy her own pillow and maybe even some sheets and definitely a fan. And some Lysol—lots of Lysol!

Sunday night will be different. I'll be able to get some sleep, she thought, hoping the rowdiness of the neighborhood could be attributed to the weekend.

She fell into an exhausted sleep only to be awakened by a loud banging on her door.

"Hey, Sid. Open up," a man's voice said.

Brianna sat up, hardly daring to breathe, hoping he would go away when no one answered. She was glad the door had a deadbolt and a chain lock.

"Come on, Sid. Lemme in." The man continued pounding on the door.

"Sid's not here," Brianna said, giving up on the idea he was just going to go away.

"Whoa, Sid. You got a girl in there? Way t'go, Sid. Hey, Tommy. Sid's got hisself a girl."

"Aw, shut up Ernie. Sid got arrested yesterday. He ain't here. Go sleep it off."

Ernie continued banging on the door.

"Girl, you wouldn't want to let ole' Ernie in, would ya'. I need a place to crash for a couple of hours. I won't be no bother."

"I've got a gun and I know how to use it," Brianna lied. "Now go away before I blow your head off."

"You're not very nice. Don't know what Sid sees in ya." Ernie stopped banging.

Brianna let out a shaky breath. After several minutes of silence she crept to the door and looked through the peep hole. A man lay slumped on the floor, probably Ernie.

She flipped on the TV on her way back to the bed. She found a station with old sitcoms. The picture was fuzzy but watchable, after a few twists of the rabbit ears.

After two episodes of *I Love Lucy* and one of *Happy Days* the sun was rising. She watched a couple more shows before her stomach growled, protesting the fact it hadn't been fed since lunch the previous day. Picking up her purse, she opened the door, leaving the chain intact. Ernie was still slumped on the floor but no one else was around and everything was blissfully quiet. Sliding the chain off, she stepped into the hallway and locked the door behind her. She tiptoed around Ernie and down the two flights of stairs, past the sleeping desk clerk and into the street. She looked around. Other than a couple of winos sleeping in doorways, the street was deserted. A convenience store sat kitty-corner and she walked toward it. She bought coffee and a donut.

"Is there a Walmart near here?" she asked the young man behind the counter.

"Yeah, a couple of blocks over on Cicero."

"Thanks." She left the store and headed in the direction the clerk had indicated, munching the donut and blowing on the scalding coffee.

* * * *

After three trips to Walmart and one to the Suds 'n' Duds, Brianna returned to her room. Armed with cleaning supplies, disinfectant and a stiff brush, she spent the next eight hours scrubbing every corner and crevice of the tiny room and adjoining bathroom until it shone—at least until it wasn't so dingy.

She stored her food in the little refrigerator, put the new sheets and pillows on the bed and hung new towels in the bathroom. She sprayed bug spray just in case and turned on the new fan for ventilation.

It was nearly dark when she sank onto the bed, exhausted but satisfied. The bed still sagged but it was clean and smelled fresh. She picked up her new prepaid cell phone and stored Mr. Sharp's number in it. She curled up on her side, clutching the phone for security and soon slept soundly.

* * * *

Brianna awoke coughing. Her eyes stung. Thick smoke filled the room. Flames flicked under the door. Still clasping the phone, she hugged the pillow to her face and climbed through the window onto the fire escape. Dropping the pillow, she grabbed the ladder, scrambling down to the third floor, then the second. She stepped onto the final ladder. An explosion knocked her to the ground.

CHAPTER FIVE

John awoke to the sound of his cell phone on the night table. He picked it up. *Two o'clock.* He glanced at the caller ID. "Cell phone, IL" it read. His irritation mounting, he punched the answer button.

"Hello."

"John Sharp?" a male voice asked.

"Yes. Who is this?"

"This is Officer Garcia of the Chicago Police. We found this phone next to a young woman who was injured in an explosion. Your number was the only one in it. She's unconscious and has no identification. Would you come down here and identify her?"

"Yes, of course. What's the address?" He scribbled the address on a pad. "I'll be there as soon as I can."

His mind raced while he dressed. What woman did he know that would be in that area at this time of the night?

When he arrived at the scene thirty minutes later, he was met by complete chaos. Yellow police tape cordoned off a wide area where fire trucks, police cars and ambulances were parked. Flames engulfed a building. Firefighters attempted to control the inferno. He parked his car and got out. He spoke to one police officer who directed him to another officer standing near an ambulance. On the curb lay a body covered with a blanket. His heart jumped to his throat.

"Officer Garcia?" he asked the man in uniform.

"Yes."

"I'm John Sharp. You need me to identify someone." He nodded toward the lifeless body. "That's not her, is it?"

"No, sir. She's in the ambulance. They'll be taking her to the hospital shortly." The officer jerked his head toward the vehicle behind him.

* * * *

Brianna opened her eyes slowly to the sound of sirens and shouting. She looked at her surroundings in the dim light. She lay on a narrow cot draped with a white sheet. An ice pack sat on her throbbing head. A plastic bag with a tube leading to a needle in her arm hung overhead. An oxygen mask covered her nose. Something encased her foot and ankle. Outside two men were talking. She saw a fire truck and policemen. The noise was deafening. *What happened?* Her vision blurred and she closed her eyes.

Something gently brushed her arm.

"Miss Ryan," a deep voice said.

Brianna opened her eyes. Mr. Sharp sat on the bench across from her. *I must be dreaming.* She closed her eyes.

"Brianna, wake up," the voice said. "The paramedics are taking you to the hospital."

Brianna opened her eyes and struggled to sit up but a strong hand on her shoulder prevented it and she hadn't the strength to resist.

"What are you doing here? I don't need a hospital. I'm fine. Just let me go home."

"The police called me. Apparently, I'm the only number in your cell phone."

Brianna groaned; a single tear trickled down her temple into her hair. "It's new."

61

"What were you doing in this neighborhood at this hour?"

"Sleeping," she stated. "I can't afford to go to the hospital. Everything I had was in there," She pointed at the burning building.

"That's where you rented a room?" He stared at her as if she'd taken leave of her senses.

She closed her eyes and nodded. John shook his head.

"You are going to the hospital. They want to take some x-rays. Insurance will cover most of it. Don't worry about the rest. Try to relax. I'll see you there." He got up, stepped to the ground, exchanged a few words with the paramedic and left.

"'Try to relax,' 'Don't worry about it,'" she sniffed. "Easy for him to say."

The medic climbed in, shut the doors and took the seat John had just vacated. He took her blood pressure, listened to her heart, checked the oxygen and IV and squeezed her big toe. When he was satisfied that she was stable he signaled the driver and the vehicle lurched forward. The IV bag swung rhythmically as sirens faded into the background. She closed her eyes again. She opened them when the paramedics set her gurney on the ground and raised it with a jolt.

They wheeled her into the emergency room, transferred her to a bed and left. She wanted to sleep but the bright overhead light made it impossible. She waited and waited for what seemed like hours. She considered leaving but she was barefoot, it was two thirty in the morning and she had nowhere to go. For the first time in her life Brianna was depressed. She was alone, hurt, tired and homeless. With all her money literally gone up in smoke, she was destined to remain that way. And now she would have a hospital bill on top of everything else. She cried giant tears.

She wiped her eyes on a corner of the sheet that covered her and glanced around the stark, green-curtained enclosure for tissues. She finally spotted a box on a stainless steel tray across the room. Desperately needing to blow her nose, she sat up, scooted past the guard rails to the end of the bed and swung her legs over the edge, sliding until her feet touched the cold tile floor. Intense pain shot up her leg when she put her weight on it. The room tilted. She lurched at the tray and it crashed to the floor, taking her with it. Suddenly the tiny cubicle filled with people that seemed to materialize from the curtains. Through an opening she could see a man in a white coat talking with a tall man wearing gray pants and a black polo shirt. *Mr. Sharp? Why is he here?*

"I need a tissue," she said.

"We'll get you one," said one of the green-clad people as they picked her up, laid her back on the bed and raised the side rails.

"Thank you," she said as a nurse handed her the tissues. She blew her nose.

Her eyes locked on Mr. Sharp as he conversed with the other man.

"I'm sorry. Unless you are family I can't give you any information," the man said to Mr. Sharp.

"He's my husband." She looked around. Had those words tumbled from her mouth? Apparently the connection between her brain and tongue had been completely severed but the thought of a familiar face made her feel a little better.

The man and Mr. Sharp simultaneously turned toward her. The doctor raised a skeptical eyebrow while Mr. Sharp just stared at her as if she'd lost her mind. Brianna blushed. They spoke a few more seconds before approaching her.

"Hello. I'm Dr. Holloway," he said, shining a penlight in her eye. "I was telling your, uh, husband—"

Brianna flicked an embarrassed glance at her boss. He stood with his arms crossed and a grave look fixed on her.

"—I don't think it's anything serious. We're going to take some x-rays and a CT scan just to make sure. You're a very lucky young lady." The doctor patted her shoulder, spoke to John and disappeared through the curtain.

"Lucky? Hmfp," she grumbled.

"He's right. You're lucky you weren't killed. I saw a couple of people who weren't so lucky. What in the world possessed you to get a room in that building, in that neighborhood?"

"I don't want to talk about it. I just want to go ho… somewhere." Tears clouded her eyes as she remembered she didn't have a home to go to.

"You don't want to talk about it. Well, young lady, you are going to have to talk about it whether you want to or not. I don't know what I'm going to do with you."

"Stop talking like you're my father." She met his eyes. "It's not— **I'm** not your problem. I can take care of myself."

"Yes, you're doing a smashing job so far." A smile twitched the corners of his mouth.

Brianna glared at him and opened her mouth but an orderly stepped into the room to take her to radiology before she could say something she would most likely regret.

* * * *

Mr. Sharp sat in the cubicle sipping a cup of coffee when she returned.

"Why are you still here? Actually, why were you even here in the first place?"

"The police called me. I told you in the ambulance."

"You were in the ambulance?"

"You don't remember?"

Brianna shook her head. "Well, you can go now. I'll be fine."

The doctor returned. He shuffled through papers on a chart before looking up.

"Just as I suspected, you have a mild concussion and a badly sprained ankle. We'd like to keep you overnight for observation. I'll see about getting you a room." John left the room with the doctor and returned a few seconds later.

"Where am I?" Brianna asked.

"Mercy Medical," John answered.

Brianna groaned.

"Don't they usually take indigents to Cook County? I can't stay here."

"Where do you plan to go?"

Brianna looked down at her hands as they twisted the sheet. She had nowhere to go. She looked up at Mr. Sharp.

"I - don't - know," she said, tears trickling down her cheeks.

He handed her a tissue, looked at her intently and stroked his chin.

"Since you declared yourself my wife, I guess I should take you home with me."

Her head jerked up and she stared at him.

"You most certainly will not."

"Unless there is someone else you can call you're stuck with me. The doctor says you can't be left alone for 24 hours."

"I'll call Carly. She'll take care of me. Where's my phone?"

John reached into his pocket, retrieved the phone and handed it to her. She took the phone, looked at it for several seconds, then looked back at Mr. Sharp.

"I can't remember her number," Brianna said, tears welling in her eyes again.

She handed the phone back to him as the doctor re-entered the room.

"We have a room all ready for you. Someone will take you up shortly," he said.

67

"I'll not be staying."

"I'm afraid my wife can be quite stubborn at times," John said, moving to her side and placing an arm around her shoulders, drawing a mutinous glare from Brianna. He smiled down at her. "If it's okay with you, I'll take her home. She'll rest better there."

The doctor looked from John to Brianna, then back to John. "Well, okay but I want her to see her doctor on Monday. In the meantime, keep the foot elevated with an ice pack – fifteen minutes every hour or two. And, most importantly, wake her every two hours for the next twenty-four. Make sure she is not disoriented, or nauseated. If she is, bring her back in here immediately. Some short-term memory loss and mood swings are normal."

"You can count on it, Dr. Holloway," John said shaking his hand. "And, thank you for everything."

"I'll send someone in with a splint and a wheelchair."

"That's not necessary," Brianna said.

"Hospital policy." Turning to John, he said, "Bring your car up to the entrance, she'll be right out."

"I'm not your wife," Brianna stated when the doctor left.

"Hey, you said it, not me," he laughed.

"The words just sort of fell out," she sighed. "I don't know why you bothered. I'm just another employee and a rather bothersome one at that."

He smiled. "Everyone needs a helping hand occasionally."

"Yeah, the 'luck of the Irish' seems to have abandoned me."

"So it seems." He smiled, brushed a strand of hair from her forehead and added, "But I won't."

A young male nurse came in with a wheelchair, a pair of crutches and a splint. John left to get the car. The nurse placed the canvas and plastic contraption around her foot and leg fastening it with Velcro straps.

"Ready to go?" He asked, helping her off the gurney and into the chair. Brianna blinked back more tears and nodded, wiping her eyes with the back of her hand.

Mr. Sharp and the nurse helped her into his silver Mercedes. The crutches were stowed in the backseat. She leaned her head on the soft, gray leather headrest and closed her eyes.

* * * *

Brianna woke with a start when a hand touched her shoulder. She rolled onto her back, blinked and squinted in the dimly lit room until she focused on a tall figure standing beside the bed. She sat up with a groan, slowly piecing together the jumbled events of the past night.

"How are you feeling?" She recognized the deep voice of her boss. *He's everywhere.*

"Much better than I smell, I'm sure." She wrinkled her nose at the lingering, acrid odor of smoke surrounding her. The slight smile he gave her caused her heart to summersault. *Damn! He's going to give me a heart attack if he keeps doing that.* She gulped. Even a half-smile brought a twinkle to his eyes.

"Seriously, Miss Ryan, does your head ache? Are you nauseated?"

"No, I'm actually kind of hungry."

"That's a good sign." He smiled again, turned and left the room leaving the door slightly ajar.

Brianna surveyed her surroundings. Soft, gray walls, silver plush carpet she longed to sink her toes into, a wall of muted multi-colored silk drapes that matched the duvet on the queen-sized bed. The wall opposite the bed had two doors, one of which she hoped was a desperately needed bathroom. She debated for three seconds whether to attempt the trip on her own or call for help. Her pride chose the former.

She swung her feet to the floor, reveling for a moment in the luxurious carpet. Her toes were not disappointed. Reaching for the crutches leaning against a small bedside chair, she stood up, adjusted the crutches under her arms and headed for the closest door. It was a walk-in closet. The door on the other end of the dresser was a bathroom. She caught her reflection in the large mirror above the white marble vanity. Her hair looked like it had a fight with a food processor and lost. She wore a Notre Dame football jersey – *only* a football jersey. She stared into the mirror, the black jersey accented the paleness of her complexion. The realization hit her as to the only possible explanation of how it came to be on her. A flush warmed her cheeks and flooded her body.

She re-entered the bedroom and saw her clothes, clean and neatly folded on the corner of the bed. She sat down next to them just as Mr. Sharp came in carrying a tray laden with a small teapot and cup, a glass of orange juice and a bagel spread with strawberry cream cheese.

"I assumed you would prefer tea but I can make coffee if you'd like."

"Tea is perfect. I can come out to the kitchen to eat." She picked up her clothes and hugged them to her chest, avoiding his eyes.

"You can come out for lunch. You need more rest."

When she was settled back in the bed he set the tray across her lap and poured her tea. "Do you want cream or sugar?"

Brianna nodded her head, wincing slightly at the movement. He looked at her through narrowed eyes while adding the condiments to her cup.

"Are you sure you're all right?" He asked as he sat in the small chair.

"I'm okay." She stared at the mirror above the dresser. It would be so much easier to eat if he wasn't watching her.

"Something is wrong. One of the first things I noticed about you, and admired, by the way, is you always look me in the eye and now you're not."

She took a drink of juice and briefly glanced at him, feeling the flush cover her again.

"It's just that– well– it's kind of embarrassing." She plucked at the jersey.

"My old football jersey is embarrassing?" His eyes furrowed.

"No, but how I came to be wearing it is." She glowered at him.

John laughed. "You think I put it on you?"

"I can't imagine how else I got it on."

"You mean you really don't remember?"

His look of concern confused her. She shook her head.

"I assure you, Miss Ryan, I did not put that jersey on you. You wanted to take a shower when we got here but didn't have anything clean to put on. I gave you that. When I came back in you were sound asleep. Your dirty clothes were in a pile on the bathroom floor so I washed them."

"Thank you."

"You're welcome. Eat your breakfast and get some more rest. I'll be in the living room right outside your door." He rose and walked to the door.

"You didn't have to give me your room. I'd be perfectly happy on the sofa," she said.

He turned back and smiled, "This is the guest room, Miss Ryan. Get some rest. I'll be back for the tray."

* * * *

Brianna sat on the wide seat in the shower and rinsed the shampoo from her hair, hopefully sending the remnants of the smoky residue down the drain. She stepped out of the shower, dried and wrapped a towel around her wet head. A terry bathrobe hung on the back of the door. She hobbled over and shrugged into it.

"Ahhh," she exclaimed as she opened the door and hopped on one foot to the bed.

"Is something wrong?" John called through the partially closed door.

"I just remembered Carly's number. Where's my phone?"

He opened the door and crossed to the dresser, retrieved the phone and handed it to her. He left her alone to make the call.

Brianna quickly tapped in the numbers and saved it to her contact list before she forgot it again. She wiggled her toes in the carpet while she waited for Carly to answer.

"Carly, it's Bree," she said when the call connected. She barely gave Carly a chance to respond before launching into the events of the last two days. "Could I stay with you again until I can find another room?" She listened to the response. Her shoulders slumped as she disconnected and laid the phone on the bed beside her. Bracing her hands on either side of her, she watched her foot swing lightly across the carpet.

"Come in," she responded to the knock on the door.

"Were you able to reach your friend?" John asked as he crossed to the bedside chair and sat.

Brianna nodded without looking up.

"And?" He prompted.

She took a deep breath and met his gaze.

"She's out of town. Rob's parents invited them up to their lake home in Wisconsin for a week. They won't be back 'til Saturday night." She sighed. "Now what am I going to do? All my clothes are there and I have nowhere to go — again." Her shoulders drooped and she focused on her feet.

After a few seconds John spoke. "You can stay here. You are my wife, after all."

Brianna jerked her head up, deep red staining her cheeks. "You're not going to let me live that one down, are you?"

John shook his head, amusement gleaming in his eyes. "Nope."

"Seriously, I can't impose on you. Besides, can you imagine the gossip at work if it got out? No, I'll figure something out." What, she didn't know.

"It's really no imposition, Miss Ryan. We won't worry about the gossip. You're not going to work this week anyway."

"I can't afford to take a whole week off. I already owe you one paycheck. If I lose another week's pay I'll never be able to afford my own place."

"You don't owe me anything. You have sick leave coming. I have plenty of room and, when you're well, we'll look for a place for you. Now, let's get that foot up and put some ice on it."

She swung her legs onto the bed and leaned back on the pillows.

"Do you need anything else?" John asked before he left to get an ice pack.

Brianna shook her head and closed her eyes.

* * * *

Early Monday morning John knocked on Brianna's door. She groaned and pulled the covers up around her neck before telling him to come in.

"I'm leaving for the office now," he said, setting a small breakfast tray on the nightstand. "My housekeeper, Mrs. Miller, will be here at nine o'clock. She'll fix your lunch and help you with anything you need. Make an appointment with your doctor and let me know the time. I'll drive you."

"I don't have a doctor," Brianna said, attempting to sweep the unruly mass of curls away from her eyes.

John looked at her for a moment before speaking. "I'll make one with mine. What's your cell number?"

Brianna gave him the number wondering why all men had to be so bossy. She would have argued but instinctively knew it wouldn't do any good. Besides, she did need to see a doctor and his was likely one of the best.

After he left, she hobbled to the bathroom and back. Settling into the bedside chair, she added cream and sugar to the tea. She nibbled a piece of dry wheat toast. Who eats dry toast, she thought and dunked it into the tea.

Mrs. Miller, a slightly plump, older woman with graying hair and a warm smile arrived promptly at nine o'clock. After she introduced herself, she bustled off to the kitchen.

* * * *

Brianna's eyes fluttered open at the sound of her name. Mrs. Miller stood beside her bed with a tray.

"I'm sorry to wake you, dear but Mr. Sharp called and said he would be here to pick you up at one. It's nearly noon now. I've brought your lunch."

Brianna sat up and Mrs. Miller set the tray across her lap.

"I didn't realize I had fallen asleep," she said pushing the hair out of her eyes. "This looks delicious. You shouldn't have gone to so much trouble for me."

"No trouble, Miss."

"Well, thank you. You're very kind." Brianna bit into the chicken salad sandwich.

CHAPTER SIX

Unable to keep his thoughts from drifting, John turned his chair toward the window. Resting his elbows on his knees, he steepled his fingers under his chin and looked down at the tiny sail boats gliding on the lake across the street. He envisioned Brianna on the deck, the wind teasing her hair, water glistening on her bikini clad... Leaning back in his chair he inhaled deeply. *I do not get involved with employees.* But... He jumped and turned his chair when someone coughed.

"I didn't mean to startle you. I did knock." Kaitlyn stood by his desk. "How about taking me to lunch?"

He glanced at his watch. "I'm sorry, Kaitlyn, I can't. I have an appointment."

"Your loss." Kaitlyn pouted. "I have some shopping to do anyway. I haven't a thing to wear."

John doubted that. He stood nearly knocking over his chair.

"Thanks, Kaitlyn." He flashed her a smile.

"For what?" Kaitlyn looked puzzled as John rushed past her and out the door.

* * * *

John let himself into his apartment and greeted Mrs. Miller as she came out of Brianna's room with a lunch tray.

"Is she awake?" he asked.

"Yes, sir."

"I'm awake and ready to go," Brianna said from her room. When he entered, she raised her feet, one sporting the clunky boot splint and the other a floppy sock tied on with a black shoelace. "Mrs. Miller gave me this sock. I hope you don't mind."

John shook his head with a slight smile.

"It did occur to me that you may need a few things. Do you feel up to a little shopping after your doctor's appointment?"

"Shopping? In case you've forgotten, I don't have any money." She frowned at him.

80

"Don't worry about it. You need clothes and things, don't you?" She shrugged. "Where would you like to go? Bloomingdales? Nordstrom's?"

Her eyes widened. "Right. How about Goodwill?"

He put his hands on his hips. "I don't think so. What about Target?"

Brianna locked her eyes with his, "Walmart." She stood as tall as she could on one leg.

John narrowed his eyes and set his jaw. "Target."

Brianna opened her mouth to protest and closed it again. No sense arguing with him. It was, after all, his money. She'd figure out some way to repay him but for now it appeared she didn't have a choice.

* * * *

The car waited by the front door when they exited the building. The doorman reached to open her door and John helped her into the passenger seat.

"Seat belt?" he asked as he slid behind the wheel.

"Yes, Dad."

A brief smile softened his features. He was an incredibly good-looking man but, when he smiled, even briefly, he was devastating. He has lots of nice features, she thought. She wanted to run her fingers through the thick brown hair and mess it up a little. He had a straight nose and well-shaped lips that made hers itch just looking at them. She wondered what they would feel like against hers. She shook her head and shivered. She must have hit her head harder than she realized. *Get a grip on yourself. You are not looking for a new relationship. Besides, he's out of your league!*

"Are you cold?" John asked, noticing her shiver.

"No, I'm fine. It's a beautiful day. I love spring. The leaves are out and everything is green again."

"They are, aren't they? I hadn't really noticed. Green is nice." He smiled. She smiled back and suppressed another shiver.

"Have you always lived in Chicago?" Brianna asked.

"I grew up in Evanston. My parents were professors at Northwestern."

"But you went to Notre Dame?" she asked.

"I did," he said.

"Do they still live here?"

"No."

"Oh. What'd they teach?"

"Dad taught history and Mother taught Medieval English Literature. You certainly ask a lot of questions."

"My dad always said, 'If you want to know something, ask.' Since we're living together, I figured I should know a little more about you."

John cast her an amused look.

Brianna blushed. "Well, not *together* together. I didn't... I mean... Oh, never mind."

John laughed. "Must have been a Freudian slip."

Color flooded her face.

They pulled into the parking lot of the medical building.

* * * *

"You didn't have to come in with me," Brianna said, seated on the exam table. "I'm not a child."

"I want to know what he says and I'm not sure you would tell me."

Brianna opened her mouth but the doctor came in and she swallowed her retort.

John sat in the corner while the doctor poked and prodded Brianna.

"Everything looks good under the circumstances," Dr. Anderson said to John as he strapped on her splint. "She can put some weight on it when she's wearing the splint. Alternate heat and ice for twenty minutes every three to four hours. Take Tylenol for pain as needed. She'd probably do better with a quad-cane. It's easier to manage than crutches."

John stood up and extended his hand, "Thanks, Dave. I appreciate your seeing her on such short notice."

"I'd like to see her again in a week. Let me know if she has any headaches, blurry vision or dizziness during the week," the doctor said. "I'm sure she'll be fine."

John turned and helped Brianna off the exam table, handing her the crutches.

While she adjusted the crutches under her arms, John chatted with the doctor. She ignored their conversation.

"Thanks." Swinging through the door John held for her, she smiled at the doctor. She ignored John completely. She stood to the side while he made an appointment for the following week.

She stared straight ahead on the short drive to Target, giving one word answers to his questions.

"Is something bothering you?" John asked.

Brianna gave him a cool glance. "Whatever makes you think that?" She turned her attention back to the road.

"Oh, I don't know, maybe two 'fine's' and a 'whatever' have something to do with it. Didn't you like Dr. Anderson?"

For once in her life, Brianna thought before she spoke. How was she going to say what she wanted to without sounding churlish, childish and ungrateful?

"Dr. Anderson was okay. You, on the other hand—,"

"Me? What did I do?"

"I don't mean to be rude but you're kind of, umm, bossy. Actually, you're very bossy. You remind me of my father. Everyone knows what's best for me but me. I was the patient, the one injured but you two talked like I wasn't even there or capable of understanding the complexities of my condition. I'm not stupid, you know."

John honked the horn, slammed on the brakes and threw his arm in front of Brianna all at the same time.

"Damn! I wish people would pay attention to their driving instead of talking on cell phones," he glanced at Brianna. "Are you all right?"

She nodded, struggling to regain her breath.

* * * *

"Those crutches will just be in the way. Hop to that bench while I park the car," John said, stopping in front of the Target entrance.

"Yes, boss," she mumbled as she got out of the car, gained her balance and slammed the car door. She chided herself for being ungrateful but, boy, did she hate being told what to do. She passed the bench and limped into the store, decided on an electric scooter and drove off just as John entered the store. He shot her a chastising look. She grinned, did a 360 around him and sped off in the direction of the clothing department.

Just a few necessities, she thought, pulling a Tweety Bird nightshirt off the rack and tossing it into the basket. A six pack of bright bikini underwear, a bra, two T-shirts and a pair of jeans followed. She zipped off to the toiletries. She tossed in some deodorant, a toothbrush and toothpaste, a hairbrush, a detangling comb, and some elastic ponytail holders. John dropped bottles of strawberry scented shampoo and conditioner into the basket. She looked up at him and smiled. He smiled back. She nearly ran the cart into an elderly woman. She reversed and almost ran over John's foot. She glared at him when he chuckled.

Brianna drove down another aisle, picked some strawberry flavored lip balm and announced, "I'm done."

John pointed at the large sock on her foot.

"A pair of shoes might be a good idea."

"Oh, right." She executed a sharp U-turn and headed to the shoe section.

She grabbed a pair of orange flip-flops and tossed them on top of the pile. John frowned and picked up a pair of sturdy athletic shoes.

"Not my size," Brianna said.

"Well, find some that are your size because I'm not letting you out of here with only those things. They're dangerous," he said, pointing at the flip-flops.

Brianna hesitated, giving him a mutinous glance. John crossed his arms and refused to budge. She gave in, again, and found a pair of red plaid sneakers in her size and dropped them triumphantly into the basket. John shook his head.

When she reached the checkout, John waited for her. He tossed a bottle of purple nail polish onto the conveyor belt.

She added a bottle of polish remover. Their eyes locked.

He chose a pack of gum.

She picked up a candy bar.

He reached for a magazine.

"Enough, already. These aren't necessary." She leaned forward and unloaded her basket, blocking John's attempt to help. John tossed two magazines onto the pile. Brianna rolled her eyes and headed for the exit.

She waited several minutes before turning back to the checkout counter. John was laughing with the cute, young clerk who beamed her best, metal enhanced smile at him.

"Are you about done here?" Brianna asked.

John gathered up the bags and caught up to her at the exit.

"I thought you were over being mad at me. Now, I'm not so sure," John said.

"I'm not mad."

John attempted to help her off the scooter but she shook her arm free. She hopped off and hobbled out the door ahead of him.

"No, you're not mad," John followed her to the sidewalk.

She got as far as the curb and stopped. How was she going to manage the curb without landing on her butt in the gutter?

John approached but refrained from offering his assistance.

"Wait here. I'll get the car." He dug the keys from his pocket and walked the short distance to the car.

He pulled up in front of Brianna and leaned across the passenger seat to open the door but she jerked it open before he reached the handle. She'd barely fastened her seatbelt when he took off with a jolt only to stop abruptly before entering the street. She glanced at him out of the corner of her eye taking note of the clenched jaw and tight lips. She took a deep breath, drawing his attention.

"I'm sorry." She gave him a timid smile. "I guess I'm a little tired and my ankle hurts but that's no excuse for being rude or ungrateful for all you've done."

John didn't answer but his features relaxed. He pulled into a strip mall a short distance away.

"I'll just be a minute," he said, opening his door.

Brianna watched as he entered a medical supply store. *Okay, now I really feel bad. How can I be so grumpy when he's being so nice? It doesn't bother me that a teenager practices her flirting on him. Yes, it does, but it shouldn't.* She closed her eyes, leaning her head back on the headrest. *He's my boss, my bossy boss.*

He returned in a few minutes with a quad-cane, stowing it on top of the crutches in the back seat.

"Thank you," she said, tears inexplicably clouding her eyes.

"You're welcome," he stated with a smile which she returned before averting her eyes to look out the side window. *Bossy boss, bossy boss. Damn!*

He surprised her when he reached over and patted her hand as it lay on the console.

"We'll be home in a couple of minutes. You can rest while I reheat the dinner Mrs. Miller left for us."

Brianna, unable to speak through the lump in her throat, could only nod.

The drive to John's condo took only fifteen minutes but to Brianna, it felt like an eternity. She leaned her head on the headrest and watched buildings and cars pass the window.

Her conflicting emotions disturbed her. A cry baby one second and a shrew the next - not like her normal, cheerful self at all. He glanced at her and smiled before returning his attention to the road. Her heart raced. She wasn't sure if she liked this feeling either. Well, actually, she did like the feeling, it was just… impossible. He was her boss and off limits. The last thing she needed in her life right now was more complications. Turning her head back to the side window, she wiped her eyes with the back of her hand when the incessant tears threatened again.

John pulled up in front of his building, leaving the engine running as he exited. The valet waited while he helped Brianna out. Handing her the new cane, he turned back to retrieve the packages.

"We'll donate the crutches to a free clinic," he said, taking her arm to steady her as she limped to the entrance aided by the cane.

Once in the elevator, he let go of her arm. The warmth lingered as a reminder of his touch. She released a long sigh.

"You must be worn out," he said, as the elevator doors opened. "Go lie down and I'll find the heating pad for your ankle."

Exhausted, more from the emotional upheaval than the physical activity, she didn't argue. Limping to the bed, she sat on the edge to remove the now dirty sock and the splint before swinging her legs onto the bed. John came in a few minutes later carrying a heating pad under his arm, a glass of water in one hand and a bottle of pain reliever in the other. He reached behind the night stand to plug in the heating pad, his head so close she could smell his after-shave. Inhaling deeply, she closed her eyes and lay back on the pillow.

"Sit up and take these," he said, shaking two tablets from the bottle. She rose on one elbow and opened her mouth. He dropped the pills in and handed her the water. Moving to the foot of the bed, he carefully picked up her foot, gently placed it onto the heating pad and switched it on low. Her eyes closed.

CHAPTER SEVEN

Brianna awoke to total darkness and complete silence. It took a few seconds to get her bearings before switching on the bedside lamp. She leaned down to turn off the heating pad. It was already off, though still warm. Noticing the packages on the dresser, she sat up, reached for the cane and hobbled over to put away the items. After putting the toiletries in the bathroom, the jeans, shirts and shoes in the closet, she returned to gather the items that needed washing and discovered an extra bag. Reaching inside, she pulled out a sundress.

Clutching the dress, she tottered as fast as her cane would allow, in search of her benefactor. Entering the darkened living room, she saw a light coming from a room in the opposite corner and headed toward it.

"What's this?" she said, holding up the dress as if it were contaminated.

John looked up from the book he was reading.

"I believe it's a dress."

"I know it's a dress. It isn't a necessity."

"Does everything have to be a necessity? The green matched your eyes so I bought it. We can take it back if you don't like it"

"I didn't say I didn't like it. I can't afford it."

"It's a gift, Brianna. Say 'thank you.'"

"Thank you, Mr. Sharp."

"John."

Brianna looked startled. "Excuse me."

"You can call me 'John.' Mr. Sharp and Miss Ryan seem a little formal under the circumstances, don't you think?"

She swallowed, then stammered, "Well, yes. I suppose it is but only here. You're still 'Mr. Sharp' at work."

John laughed. "I somehow didn't figure you for a strict protocol type person." He lowered his feet from the hassock and stood up. "I hope you're hungry because I'm starved. Put the dress on while I see about dinner."

She watched him walk to the kitchen before heading to her room to try on the dress. *He waited to have dinner with me.* A feeling of elation surged through her.

* * * *

Brianna crossed the long, narrow kitchen taking note of the tall cherry cabinets above the black granite countertops. She sat on a stool at the small peninsula bar while John heated the dinner Mrs. Miller had left for them.

"You're not a shark — I mean, you're much nicer—"

John faced her and raised one eyebrow. Brianna felt the blush travel up from the low 'V' of her neckline and settle onto her cheeks.

"I mean you're different than you are at work." She looked down and traced the pattern of the granite countertop with her fingernail. When she looked up he smiled.

She watched as John took dishes out of the refrigerator and set them on the countertop. He put the lasagna in the microwave. While it heated, he uncovered a mixed green salad and set bottles of dressing beside it.

"Anything I can do?" Brianna asked.

"I've got it," John replied, getting plates and bowls from the cabinet followed by silverware from a drawer.

He removed the lasagna and wrapped several slices of buttered French bread in paper towels placing them in the microwave. Reaching into the wine cooler under the counter, he pulled out a bottle of red wine, then put it back in.

"Probably not a good idea under the circumstances," he said, looking at Brianna.

"Not for me but you go ahead. I'll just have water or juice, if you have any."

"I do. What would you like, orange, apple or cranberry?"

"Apple's fine."

He poured juice into two stemmed wine glasses before serving their food.

"Where would you like to eat? Here? The dining room? How about the terrace?"

"The terrace would be lovely." She answered. The kitchen suddenly seemed warm.

The lake caught, shimmered and reflected the moon and stars. John leaned back in his chair, captivated by the copper highlights dancing in Brianna's hair as a slight breeze lifted the silky strands. Brianna ran a hand over her hair, smoothing the wayward curls and shivered.

96

"You must be chilly," John rose and extended his hand to assist her. "I'll clear the dishes. I'll give you a tour of the condo if you're feeling up to it."

"I'd like that."

John gathered the dinnerware and took it to the kitchen. Brianna hobbled after him. She leaned heavily on her cane as she watched him. When he'd finished, he gestured for her to lead the way through a doorway between the peninsula and the door to the terrace. He offered his hand as she negotiated the step down from the black marble tile to the silver plush carpet of the large sunken room that served as both living room and dining room.

"Did you take these photos?" She said, pointing to a group of black and white photographs on the wall opposite the fireplace. "They're quite good."

"I did, thank you. That's about the only thing I had to do with this room."

Brianna looked at him quizzically.

He continued past the teak dining table surrounded by six straight backed chairs covered in dove gray fabric.

"I had a party a couple of years ago. Kaitlyn gave me her decorator's number. Apparently my condo wasn't up to her standards."

"These glass sculptures are colorful." Brianna ran a finger over the artwork on the lighted shelves that flanked the white marble fireplace.

John picked up a blue vase, reminiscent of waves.

"This is the only piece I picked out. I bought it at a little gallery in Hawaii."

"It's beautiful," she said. It was the only piece she really liked.

She glanced at the large painting above the mantel.

"I'm not a big fan of modern art but it does add color to the room." John said. "I have to wonder what they were thinking when they painted it."

"I imagine they were feeling more that thinking."

John studied the painting and stroked his chin. "Okay. What was he feeling?"

"Modern art is very subjective, much more so than other paintings like a landscape or still-life. It invokes different feelings in different people. This one makes me feel the artist's anger."

"Really? How so?"

"His liberal use of bold red slashes– red always seems angry– at least to me. The purple lines are a transition to the blue. The purple represents confusion and the blue denotes peace. He used much more purple than blue so, I'm guessing he was more confused than at peace when he painted this." She smiled up at John who appeared to be interested so she continued. "He used a small sunburst of yellow in that corner probably representing hope. To me he was angry but wanted peace and he had a small ray of hope so all was not lost."

"You got all that from this?" He swept his hand in front of the painting.

"Or, it could be that he just liked bold colors or was higher that a kite." She grinned.

John laughed.

They passed the long and sleek charcoal ultra suede sofa flanked by four white chairs. Glass topped teak tables with contemporary brushed stainless lamps completed the room. An entire wall of floor to ceiling windows with access to the terrace framed the dining area. John pressed a button on the wall. Silver silk draperies slowly moved across the windows obscuring the sparkling lake.

They continued into the den where the décor was a dramatic contrast to the living room. Walnut paneling covered the walls. Book shelves lined the end wall and another long one, broken up by an antique credenza. A large seascape hung above it.

Brianna ran a hand lightly over the frame of the painting.

"I love Winslow Homer. This is an original, isn't it?"

John nodded. "My great-grandfather bought it shortly after the Civil War before Homer became famous." He picked up a remote control and pushed a button. A large, flat screen television descended from the ceiling in front of the painting. He opened drawers that housed numerous DVD's and showed her how to use the player and sound system. "That should keep you entertained while you're convalescing."

An over-stuffed loveseat faced the TV. A matching chair and ottoman sat at an angle. Heavy wood end tables held antique brass lamps that cast a warm glow in the room. A desk with a computer occupied the area in front of another wall of windows that could be covered by deep blue drapes.

He led her through the living room, assisting her up the step to the entry level. He pointed out the half bath and a utility room off the entry hall, opposite the kitchen, before continuing past her bedroom to a set of double doors.

He held the door open, suggesting she should precede him into the room. Another windowed wall opposite the door drew her eyes to the moonlight streaming across the king sized bed. John turned on a bedside lamp casting a soft glow. She forced her gaze away from the black damask striped duvet. Cobalt accents softened the stark masculinity of the room. He continued into the master bath. Brianna's eyes widened. It was nearly as big as Carly's whole apartment. John brought her attention to a large black tub. It sat on a raised platform under the corner windows that framed the city skyline.

"I thought you might want to use this. It would help your ankle." He showed her how to turn on and adjust the multiple jets and water temperature. "Feel free to use it anytime." He smiled.

Brianna felt as if she could melt onto the marble floor.

CHAPTER EIGHT

After finally getting a full night's sleep, Brianna woke early. She slipped into her robe and went to the kitchen. The condo was quiet which meant John was either not up or already gone - most likely the latter.

She found a box of Honey Nut Cheerios in the pantry and poured a bowl, adding milk. Perching on a bar stool at the peninsula to eat, Brianna opened the newspaper that lay on the counter.

John entered the room dressed in his workout clothes, a towel draped around his neck, his tousled hair falling across his brow. Brianna inhaled a mouthful of cereal and spewed it across the countertop and newspaper. John quickly crossed the room and thumped her back while she coughed and struggled to regain her breath.

"Okay?" John asked when she finally stopped coughing.

Brianna nodded. "Sorry, I kind of messed up your paper. You startled me. I thought you'd gone to work."

"I leave for work at seven-thirty. I work out from six to seven."

Brianna filed the information away for future reference.

John moved to the other side of the bar which made breathing infinitely easier for her. She appreciated the play of muscles in his bare arm as he took a cup from the cupboard and filled it with coffee, offering her one. She shook her head. Probably best to keep my mouth empty, she thought.

He put an English muffin - whole wheat - into the toaster while she cleaned up the mess she'd made. When the muffin popped up he topped it with fruit spread.

He eats healthy, she thought but said, "You've got a lot of muscles for a desk jockey."

"Excuse me?" John turned with his muffin half way to his mouth.

Brianna blushed. "It's just that, normally, one wouldn't expect someone who sits behind a desk all day to have such well developed muscles. You're in really good shape."

"Thank you." He leaned against the cabinet, ankles crossed, an amused glint in his eyes, and took a bite of the muffin. He licked the jam from his lips.

Brianna looked at her bowl of soggy Cheerios and pushed it away.

After John cleared the dishes and went to take a shower, she brewed a cup of tea adding cream and sugar. She sat at the breakfast bar stirring the drink and studying the classified ads.

John returned, hair still damp but neatly combed, dressed in a gray pinstripe suit with a blue shirt and blue and gray striped tie.

"Are there no affordable apartments in this city?" She looked up with a frown.

"Don't worry about it, I'm sure something will turn up" He glanced at his watch. "I have to leave now but I'll be home around six. Mrs. Miller will check on you at noon."

"Oh. Doesn't she work today?"

"No, she cleans and fixes meals for the week on Mondays. She works for others in the building the rest of the week. She's married to the night security guard. Write down her cell number in case you need anything."

Brianna scribbled the number on her napkin with a pen from the black wire desk caddy under the phone on the wall.

"There is a notepad there." He pointed to the same caddy.

She shrugged her shoulders. "This'll do. No need to waste paper."

John shook his head and smiled. "See you later. Behave yourself."

Brianna sat until she heard the front door close before she folded the newspaper and laid it on the countertop. The prospect of finding a place she could afford on her own did not look good. She glanced at the sleek, modern cabinetry with the long stainless handles that mirrored the gleaming appliances. A set of brushed stainless canisters sat next to the ceramic top stove, otherwise the granite was bare. She imagined what a few colorful accessories could do for the room. Brianna sighed. It seemed warmer when John was here.

After making her bed, she took her laundry to the utility room. She started a load and returned to her room, intending to take a shower but as she stood in front of the enclosure a picture of the large black tub floated across her mind. She secured her hair on top of her head and headed for John's bathroom.

Sunlight flooded the room and a quick glance at the bed revealed it to be neatly made. A door beside the dresser stood slightly ajar. Curiosity got the better of her and she pulled it open. Her jaw dropped as her eyes traveled around the room masquerading as a closet. It was huge, outfitted in teak and meticulous. Suits hung together in one section, shirts organized by color in another one, casual clothes in other sections. Built in shoe shelves, again, were organized by color and style. Tie carousels and drawers for socks and things completed the room. She backed out the door, careful not to disturb anything, and thought of her own chaotic closets in the past. She didn't have enough to have a chaotic closet now. She closed the door and crossed in front of the dresser to the bathroom on the other side.

Brianna turned on the water, adjusted the temperature control and the jets as John had shown her. Dropping her robe onto the fluffy white rug, she carefully mounted the step up to the tub. She noticed a bottle of strawberry bubble bath that she hadn't seen the night before. She uncapped it and added a generous amount to the rising water. Bubbles instantly grew out of the churning water, filling the tub to its brim. Brianna sank into the foamy depths and turned off the water. She placed a rolled towel behind her head and closed her eyes.

Waving a hand in front of her face as if chasing a fly from her nose, she opened her eyes. Bubbles nearly covered her head. She cleared her line of vision and saw bubbles cascading over the edge of the tub and down the steps to the floor. *Oops.* Turning off the jets and opening the drain, she struggled to stand up on the slippery surface. She looked around for something to give her some traction. Her cane was out of reach. She'd left her cell phone in her room. She would have been too embarrassed to call Mrs. Miller to help her out of the tub anyway. She waited for the tub to empty, which took awhile given the amount of foam the drain had to swallow. Finally, the water was gone. Bubbles – not so much. She shivered as she grabbed a towel and spread it on the bottom of the tub. Turning onto her knees, she used another towel to dry the rim of the tub and slowly hoisted herself up and over it. She stood there gaining her balance before attempting to reach the soggy bathrobe lying on the once fluffy white rug. It took remainder of the day to mop, launder towels and coax bubbles down a reluctant drain.

* * * *

When John arrived home, promptly at six, she greeted him wearing her one and only sundress and a smile. He returned the smile.

"I hope you weren't too bored today."

"No, not at all." Brianna replied.

She followed him into the kitchen and took her usual seat at the bar while John readied another of the meals Mrs. Miller had prepared.

"I tried out your tub today."

He removed his jacket and tie and rolled his sleeves back. "How was it?"

"Great. I loved the bubble bath. I didn't notice it last night."

"I thought you'd like it. I jogged to the corner drug store this morning instead of working out in the gym."

John opened the refrigerator and ducked his head in.

"How come you're not married or anything?" Brianna asked, while appreciating how the cut of his slacks outlined his rear.

John pulled his head out of the fridge and set the covered dish on the countertop before looking at her.

"Or, anything?" He gave her a quizzical glance.

"You'd make a great husband. I mean, you're a good looking, rich guy. You know - a good catch. And you certainly know your way around the kitchen. Women should fall all over themselves for a bit of your attention."

"You think I'm good looking?" One corner of his mouth lifted slightly.

"Well, yeah. I'm not blind."

John placed the dish in the microwave and turned it on.

"Well, I'm not rich — comfortable, but not rich."

"Very comfortable. And, you're not married because…?"

"I was." He pulled the salad and dressing from the fridge and set it in front of her.

"Oh. What happened?" Brianna added the dressing and tossed the salad.

"It didn't work out."

"Why?"

John shrugged his shoulder. "I didn't like her boyfriend." A sardonic smile curved his mouth.

"Oh." Brianna picked a cherry tomato from the salad and popped it into her mouth. "Was it recent?"

"No, about ten years ago."

"Did she live here?"

"No." John pulled the chicken casserole from the microwave.

"Why haven't you remarried?"

"You know the old saying 'once bitten....'"

Brianna inclined her head and scooped salad into the two bowls John had placed on the bar.

"I don't want to get married," she said.

"Really? And, why is that?"

"All my life people have made decisions for me. I want to make my own decisions." She noticed John's look of amusement. "I'll admit I'm not very good at it—yet. Men always have to be in control and I don't like being controlled."

"I've noticed." He flashed her one of his half smiles.

"You like living alone?" Brianna asked.

"It has its advantages."

"Like?"

He set a plate in front of her. "Like not having to answer personal questions." He tapped her nose, softening his words.

Brianna grinned, took a bite and swallowed. "I've never lived alone."

"Never?"

Brianna shook her head. "Nope. I went from my parent's to my aunt's to Eric's and now I'm here."

"Except for the time you lived at the office."

She wrinkled her nose at him. "Well, yes. I lived alone there but I didn't like it."

"So, tell me about this boyfriend that left you out on the street. Where'd you meet him?"

"We met about three years ago. He's an assistant professor in the anthropology department at the University of Chicago. I attended a class he taught on art in ancient cultures. He was very charming, blonde hair, blue eyes. One night he invited me out for coffee. We'd been dating about a year when my aunt died. He asked me to move in with him and the rest, as they say, is history."

"So, what went wrong?" John looked up from loading the dishwasher.

"Now who's being nosy?" She grinned at him. "Nothing 'went wrong' exactly, it was gradual— subtle. He started making all the decisions from where we went to who our friends were and even how I dressed. It was his idea"– She gave a derisive snicker. —"more of a command—that I switch from painting to graphic arts. He said I could make a living instead of being a 'starving artist.'"

"Ahh, I can see how that wouldn't appeal to you." He gave her a lopsided grin.

111

"Right. About six months ago I decided I'd had enough and rebelled. He didn't like that one bit."

John laughed. "That doesn't surprise me. But, not all men are like Eric, you know."

" So I've been told. It's not just Eric, my father and brothers were domineering, too. But, that's another story for another time."

* * * *

The following morning, after John left, Brianna soaked in his tub again, without bubbles. She was amazed at how much her ankle had improved. She still limped but used the cane mostly for balance.

She curled up on the loveseat in the den and lowered the TV to viewing position. After flipping through several channels something on the Food Network caught her attention. The chef showed a chicken dish with red wine sauce he would be preparing in the next segment. An idea took shape. She grabbed a pen and small note pad from the desk top. She would prepare a special dinner for John. It was easy, the chef said, which was good because she had little cooking experience. Mrs. Miller could get any groceries she needed on Friday and she'd fix the meal Saturday night.

* * * *

When Brianna entered the kitchen Saturday morning she could see John sitting at the table on the terrace reading the paper and sipping coffee. She poured a glass of orange juice and carried it outside.

John looked up. "I'm playing golf today with Dave Anderson. I'd forgotten about it until he called this morning. Do you mind being left on your own again?"

This is perfect. "No, not at all."

"I should be home around five or six."

"Great." She barely contained her excitement.

"You seem awfully anxious to get rid of me."

"Oh. No. You go on and enjoy yourself. Really. I'll be fine."

After John left, Brianna turned on the Food Network again, as if it could magically turn her into a Cordon Bleu chef. Well, a little more information couldn't hurt. She watched and absorbed as much as she could until it was time to start cooking.

She went into the kitchen, collected all the ingredients and put them on the bar. Checking her handful of notes, she gathered the necessary utensils and went to work.

* * * *

Brianna leaned on the balustrade of the balcony. The glass door behind her slid open. Straightening her spine, she took a swig of wine but didn't turn around. The hair on the back of her neck prickled as John approached. He stopped at the table and picked up the nearly empty wine bottle.

"Did you drink all of this?"

Brianna did not respond.

"Brianna?"

"No, I did not drink all that." She turned to face him.

"What the hell happened to the kitchen?" He demanded.

She gulped more wine, set the glass on the table and put her hands on her hips. "Where have you been?"

"We ran into friends at the club and had dinner." He shook his head.

Raising her chin, she said, "I fixed dinner."

"All that damage for one meal?" He swept his hand toward the kitchen.

"No, not for one meal. I cooked for you, too." Picking up her glass of wine, she turned back to the lake view.

"I brought you dinner."

114

"A phone call would have been nice." She glanced over her shoulder briefly. Draining her wine, she crossed back to the table and refilled her glass, emptying the bottle and ignoring John's scrutiny. "I worked hard planning and cooking dinner to thank you for all you've done for me and you didn't bother to come home. Do you know how hard it is to make a wine sauce?"

John picked up the empty wine bottle. "You used a two-hundred dollar bottle of wine to make a sauce?"

Brianna looked at the bottle then at John with wide eyes.

"Two-hundred dollars for a bottle of wine?" Raising the glass to her lips with a shaky hand, she turned from his gaze. "No wonder it tastes so good."

"Where's the dinner?"

"Burned. Everything was going so well. Then the pasta boiled over. While I was cleaning that up the wine sauce got lumpy. I tossed it out –" Wine sloshed as she gestured. "– and started over. When I remembered the chicken in the oven it was dry and crispy. It wasn't supposed to be dry and crispy." Her voice trailed off. "Then the sauce boiled over again."

She felt John's presence close behind her. His hand reached around, took the glass and set it on the table. He clasped her shoulders and turned her to face him. She swayed and had difficulty focusing his face.

"You haven't eaten anything, have you?" he asked.

She sluggishly shook her head. The room lurched. She reached for a chair back but John slipped an arm around her waist and guided her into the kitchen, settling her onto a barstool. He cleaned off the bar and opened a Styrofoam box, transferred the contents to a plate, heated it and set it in front of her. Brianna took one look at the grilled salmon, clasped a hand to her mouth and slid off the stool, grasping the countertop for support. She hobbled as quickly as she could to the hall bathroom and dropped to her knees in front of the commode.

She saw John's shoes in her side vision. "Go away."

John reached over her and flushed the toilet. *Oh, if only I could disappear that easily.* He wet a towel, crouched beside her and wiped her face and throat. He left the towel on the back of her neck, stood and offered his hand to help her up. Keeping a steadying arm around her, he guided her to her room and sat her on the edge of the bed.

"Are you going to be okay or do you need help?" he asked.

Brianna glared at him. Too embarrassed to show gratitude, she merely waved a hand toward the door.

John left the room. Brianna collapsed onto the pillows.

CHAPTER NINE

Brianna cautiously opened one eye, grateful for the semi-darkness of the room before opening the other one. Her head felt like an anvil someone was hammering on and she couldn't lift it. She wasn't sure what was going to explode first, her head or her bladder. Inching to the edge of the bed, she slid to her knees on the floor, resting her head on the mattress before attempting more movement. Placing both hands firmly on the bed she forced herself to her feet and limped to the bathroom.

She splashed cold water on her face before raising her head to survey her reflection. With a groan she turned away from the mirror, stripped and stepped into the shower. She sat on the wide seat trying to come up with a plan to avoid John – forever. Her brain fired off several scenarios, none of which were possible. Turning off the water, she dried and slipped into her bathrobe wrapping a towel around her head. If her head exploded it would contain the pieces.

Entering the bedroom, she saw a tray laden with a large glass of tomato juice, a small teapot and cup, dry toast and two extra strength Tylenol tablets sitting on the bed. She approached cautiously and sat beside it, tears spilling onto her cheeks. She heard a soft knock on the door.

"Come in." She wiped her eyes on the sleeve of her robe.

John poked his head in. "How are you feeling?"

She squinted through one eye. "My head's ready to explode. My stomach feels like a volcano ready to erupt. My body feels trampled by the St. Paddy's Day parade. Other than that - grand!"

He opened the door and came in, crossing to stand in front of her. Picking up the tablets and juice from the tray, he handed them to her. "This will help. Try to eat something." She swallowed the pills with a drink of juice.

"I think that bomb is going to go off any minute." She rubbed her forehead and avoided looking at him.

He put a hand under her chin, raised her head and studied her face. "I think you'll live. I'll get an ice bag for your head."

He poured a cup of tea for her before leaving the room.

Brianna drank half of the juice, nibbled a small bite of toast and sipped the tea – hot and sweet – no cream. Convinced her head wasn't actually going to blow up, she unwrapped the turban and made an effort to finger-comb her hair.

John came back with the ice pack, walked to the bathroom and returned with the detangling comb. He moved the tray to the dresser.

"Turn around." He made a circular motion with his hand. Brianna looked up at him uncertainly but did as he suggested.

She scooted around until she sat with her back to him, cross legged at the edge of the bed. John placed the comb at her hairline and drew it back. It caught on a tangle and Brianna fell against his chest. John inhaled sharply and she struggled to sit up. He steadied her with hands to her shoulders. Her pulse was anything but steady. "My mother used to comb my hair."

"I'm sure she was much better at it than I am."

"She pulled, too. The curse of curly hair, I guess."

He chuckled as he carefully drew the comb through her hair.

"Tell me about your mother."

"She was an artist."

"So that's where your talent comes from."

"I suppose but she gave it up. 'Too much real work to be done,' she said. But I think that was more my father's idea than hers. I remember when I was about five she painted a picture of me with my little dog. That's the last thing she painted. She said to me one day when I was around ten, 'Don't let anyone steal your dreams.' The light in her eyes faded and she never painted again."

"Why not?" John asked.

"I don't really know but I think my dad had a hand in that, too. One day he found her in the attic. She had destroyed all her paintings except that one. Took a butcher knife and slashed them to ribbons, she did. My dad took her to the hospital where he left her and a few months later he sent me to live with my aunt and uncle here in Chicago. I was fourteen. He said they didn't have time for my shenanigans, besides it wasn't right for me to be raised by five grown men."

"How long was she in the hospital?"

"A couple of years but by then I was in school here so they left me be."

"That must have been hard for you. Is she all right now?"

"Oh, yes. She's fine. It was one of those change of life breakdowns not handled well by a bunch of men."

"And the painting? Do you still have it?"

"I did but Eric took it along with some I had done. They're not worth anything to anyone else. I don't know why he would want them."

He gently finished combing her hair. When she laid down, he put the ice bag on her head, turned off the bedside lamp and walked to the door.

"Thank you." She closed her eyes.

"Anytime." He eased the door shut.

* * * *

Several hours later, Brianna wandered onto the terrace where John sat on one of the loungers reading. A gallon of sun tea brewed on the table. She took a seat on the chaise next to his.

"I'm sorry about the dinner and the wine and – everything," she said, watching white clouds drift across the early afternoon sky.

John put his book down.

"Don't worry about it. I appreciate the thought." He turned toward her. "I read online this morning about Red Wine Headache syndrome. Surprisingly, it's a fairly common reaction. That and the fact you hadn't eaten anything is probably what made you sick. You really didn't drink enough to cause a bad hangover."

Brianna gave him a weak smile. "I suppose." It was as good an excuse as any.

"How are you feeling now? Hungry?"

"A little, I think." *If the fluttering of a thousand butterflies indicates hunger.*

John stood up. "I'll fix you a cup of soup and some crackers. That shouldn't be too hard on your stomach."

She watched him walk through the door to the kitchen appreciating the panther like combination of strength and grace. She released a long sigh. *This guy is too good to be true. I've got to be dreaming.* She pinched herself.

A few minutes later, John returned with a tray and set it across her lap. He sat on the chaise facing her,.

"When you've finished, call your friend and ask her if we can pick up your things this afternoon."

Brianna nodded and blew on the hot broth.

* * * *

Returning to her room, she picked up her cell phone and noticed a missed call and a new text message, both from Carly.

CALL ME.

Brianna pulled up her contact list. Carly's name, the first of only two contacts, was already highlighted. She pressed 'Call.'

Carly answered on the second ring.

"Hey, Carly. John…"

"John? You're on a first name basis with the boss?" Carly replied.

"Well, 'Mr. Sharp' is a little formal under the circumstances. He wants to know if we can come by and pick up my stuff today."

"You know you're welcome to stay here, Bree."

"I know but I'm all right here and, no offense, but your place is a bit small."

"Just a bit. How about I bring your clothes over? I'm dying to see you and hear everything," Carly said, her tone dripping with curiosity.

"I'll ask him if you promise to behave yourself." Asking Carly to behave was like asking her to stop breathing.

She walked to the terrace and, holding the phone against her chest, asked John, "Would it be all right if Carly brings my things over?"

"Of course. Invite her to stay for dinner, if you'd like," John said.

She relayed the message to Carly and turned off the phone.

"She said she'd love to stay since Rob is working until midnight."

"I'm sure you two have a lot to talk about."

You have no idea

"I'd like that, thank you." Brianna smiled.

"Can she manage the boxes by herself?"

"She's only bringing my clothes. There's no point in moving everything twice."

"That makes sense. What time is she coming?"

"Around four."

"I'll order a pizza or, Chinese, if you'd prefer," John offered.

"Chinese would be great."

* * * *

The doorbell rang a few minutes after four.

"I'll get it," Brianna called to John who was watching a golf tournament in the den.

Carly set the suitcases down and wrapped Bree in a bear hug as soon the door opened. Releasing her, she held her shoulders and examined her face.

"You don't look too bad under the circumstances," Carly said, smiling. She lowered her voice to a whisper. "How's life with the shark?"

"He's not a shark, Carly. I don't know how I'd have managed without him this week. He's very nice. Come on." She took Carly's hand. "I'll introduce you."

Carly hung back, taking in the living room with a low admiring whistle.

Brianna tugged at her hand.

John rose when they entered the den. Brianna made the formal introductions.

"Carly." John said, offering his hand. "Bree's told me a lot about you – all good." He smiled.

Brianna watched her normally talkative friend lose her power of speech as spots of red colored her cheeks. She hid a smile, shaking her head.

"We'll be out on the terrace," Brianna said to John, leading Carly from the room.

"Let me know when you want me to order dinner." John called after them.

Carly followed her to the kitchen and perched on a barstool while Brianna fixed two tall glasses of iced tea.

"You okay?" Brianna asked her still silent friend who now had a dreamy, far-away look on her face.

"Mmm-mmm," Carly replied, giving her head a shake. "I knew he was good looking – everyone in the office drools at the mention of his name – but up close… Wow! How do you do it?"

"Do what? Keep from drooling?" Brianna shrugged her shoulders and avoided eye contact. "I guess I'm getting used to him." The erratic pulse was a problem though.

Carly narrowed her eyes. "Yeah, right."

Brianna handed Carly a glass of tea. "Come on." She said, opening the sliding patio door.

They each sat in a chaise facing the lake and sipped their tea.

Carly sat up, set her glass on the side table and turned toward Brianna, elbows on knees, chin on hands, and leaned close. "Tell me everything."

"I've already told you everything."

"You told me about the accident but," she said, "not about him." She tossed a glance toward the den.

"There's nothing to tell, Carly. He goes to work - comes home – we eat. Maybe watch a little TV, then go to bed." Carly's eyebrows shot up. "Alone, Carly – separate rooms." Brianna swiped at her arm, knocking it off her knee.

"Where's the fun it that?" Carly swung her legs onto the chaise. "Don't you ever wonder what it'd be like to kiss him?"

All the time. "You're incorrigible, Carly and I wouldn't tell you if I did." Brianna turned her eyes to the lake.

"Ah-ha, so you do think about it."

"I do not." Brianna blushed and continued to avoid Carly's eyes.

"John and Brianna, sittin' in a tree, k-i-s-s-i-n-g." Carly chanted.

"Carly, stop it. That's not funny." Brianna rose and turned her back on her friend.

"Oh, come on. He can't hear us. Anyway, it's payback time for all the teasing I got over Rob."

"That's different. Rob was your fiancé. John's my boss."

"And roommate."

Brianna threw her an exasperated glare which Carly returned with an evil grin.

"Come on, I'll show you MY room and you can tell me all about your trip while I put my stuff away." Brianna walked stiffly through the kitchen. Picking up her suitcases by the front door, she continued to her bedroom with Carly trailing behind.

She hoisted one bag onto the bed and flipped it open. Carly perched beside it.

"Nice place," Carly said. "What's his room like?"

"It's very nice. You should see his bathroom! The tub's big enough to swim in."

That piqued Carly's interest and Brianna told her about the bubble and dinner disasters.

"It's a wonder he didn't send you packing. He must be a saint."

"Actually, he was very nice about it. The dinner, anyway. I didn't tell him about the bubbles."

"Probably a wise decision." Carly nodded. "Anything you're not telling me?"

"I'm trying to decide if your middle name is Persistent or just plain Nosy."

Carly laughed. "It's both. What are best friends for, anyway?"

Brianna sat beside her and Carly draped an arm around her shoulder giving it a squeeze.

"Truthfully Carly, I'm all mixed up inside. Sometimes I forget he's my boss. I don't need any romantic fantasies or complications right now."

"These things can't always be planned, Bree. They just happen."

"Well, nothing's happening. At least not on his side. He treats me like my brothers do, only nicer." Brianna smiled, shoved herself off the bed and finished unpacking. "He's too old for me."

"You're twenty-six and he's probably not even forty yet. That's not too old."

"He rescued me. I have a slight case of hero worship. He's not a knight in shining armor. He's…"

Carly snorted. "Just a man, I know."

"You're not helping here, Carly. He's out of my league."

"This is America, Bree. We don't have a caste system."

"You're supposed to be on my side here."

"I am on your side. I want you to be happy." She stood and held out her hand. "Come on. Show me the rest of the place – like that bathtub." She graced Brianna with her most innocent smile.

Brianna slapped at Carly's hand. They left the bedroom as John crossed the living room.

"It's nearly six. Are you ready for dinner?" he asked. Brianna nodded, Carly froze. "I'll order a variety."

"Sounds good," Brianna said. "Is it okay if I show Carly the condo?"

"Sure. Go ahead. It will probably take an hour for the food to get here." He pulled out his iPhone and looked up the number as he walked back to the den.

Brianna jerked Carly's hand. "You've got Rob. Remember?"

"Did you see the way he looked at you? He's hungry for more than food." Carly whispered.

"You have a very vivid imagination. Twisted, but vivid."

CHAPTER TEN

Brianna woke early Tuesday morning. It wouldn't do to keep John waiting. She walked into the kitchen wearing a lime green, hot pink and turquoise splash print skirt and a turquoise shirt. He was dressed in a black suit, light gray shirt and black and gray paisley tie.

"You should do something about your wardrobe," they said in unison.

"What's wrong with what I'm wearing?" they said.

They stared at each other. "You could add a little variety," Brianna said, "a little color. It would make you look friendlier, less stuffy."

"Stuffy? I run a business not a disco club."

"Okay." Brianna shrugged her shoulders. "What's wrong with what I'm wearing?"

"A little bright. I think I need sunglasses." John gestured toward the door.

"I like bright. It makes me happy." She grinned as she preceded him to the elevator.

"It's such a gorgeous day. I wish you had a convertible." Brianna said as she got into the car.

"They're not safe."

"Hmm. Don't you ever want to feel the wind blowing through your hair, enjoy life?"

"Safety is good." He made sure she fastened her seatbelt before leaving the curb. "I can 'enjoy life' and still be safe."

"What do you do for fun?" Brianna asked.

"I used to love sailing," he said. "I was interested in photography as a kid."

"You do realize you're using the past tense, don't you?" Brianna said.

"I play golf occasionally."

"Yes, I know, but that's just one thing – occasionally."

"I've been busy building a business and running a company for the last… few years."

"How many years?" she prodded.

"A few." It was her turn to raise an eyebrow. "All right, quite a few, but you don't build a successful business overnight."

"All work and no play makes Johnny a dull boy," Brianna teased.

"You think I'm dull?" She shrugged her shoulders. "I am not dull!" John stopped for a red light a block from the office.

"I think you've got potential, you've just forgotten how to play."

* * * *

Brianna spent the morning finishing the drawings for the Wildlife project. She was taking them to Mrs. Davis for approval when she ran into John.

"Are those the Wildlife drawings?" he asked. Brianna nodded. "I'll take them. I want to look them over."

"They haven't been approved yet."

He gave her an amused look. "I believe I have the authority to approve them. As I said before, I'm very impressed with them."

When she turned to walk back to her desk, several pairs of eyes followed her. *Great!*

"What was that about?" Carly asked as they were walking to the lounge for lunch.

"He just wanted the drawings I did for the wildlife account."

"Yeah, he's always coming down here to get drawings. Did you see the looks on Emily and Liv's faces? They're dying to know what's going on," Carly said.

"Yeah, I noticed, but that's all he wanted. I doubt he had an ulterior motive. I can only image what they'll make out of it. I'm starving. Let's eat?" Brianna changed the subject.

* * * *

At four-thirty Miss Davis stopped by her cubicle. "Mr. Sharp wants to see you, Miss Ryan. He wants to talk to you about the wildlife drawings. Did you give them to him without my approval? Do you think you'll win points by going over my head? We have procedures here for a reason, Miss Ryan. Nothing is to leave this office without my approval."

"Yes, Miss Davis." Brianna could see no point in arguing with her.

She said a quick good-bye to Carly. "I'll call you later." She grabbed her bag and headed for his office.

"Go on in, Miss Ryan. He's expecting you." Mr. Sharp's secretary said.

"You got me in trouble with Miss Davis," she said.

"I'm looking forward to the day that you walk in here without attacking me. Do you think that might be any time soon?" John said, standing as she approached his desk.

"I'm sorry, but she's not happy with me for going over her head to give you the drawings."

"But you didn't go over her head. I asked for them."

"You and I know that, but she doesn't. 'We have procedures here for a reason,' she said." Brianna didn't mention the looks she got from her co-workers.

"I'm sorry. I'll talk to her. I want to leave in a few minutes. Are you ready to go?"

Brianna nodded.

His phone rang. "Tell her I'll be out in a minute, Mrs. Wilson." He hung up the phone and said to her, "I'll meet you in ten minutes by the elevators downstairs."

She got up to leave just as Kaitlyn barged in.

"What's she doing here?" Kaitlyn glared at Brianna.

"She's just leaving." He addressed Brianna, "Miss Ryan, I'll see you later." He turned his attention back to Kaitlyn. "What did you want, Kaitlyn? I have to leave soon."

She watched Brianna leave then turned back to him. "You're leaving early, *again*?"

* * * *

"You seem a thousand miles away," Brianna said, joining him on the terrace. "What are you thinking about?"

"I was just counting the boats." He liked the way the moonlight cast bronze highlights on her red curls and the stars reflected in her jewel-like eyes. He reached out to touch a curl but dropped his hand before it reached its destination.

"How many are there?"

"What?"

"Boats. How many did you count?"

"Oh. I forgot," he said, still focused on her eyes.

"One of the hazards of getting older, huh?" she grinned at him.

John laughed, "You talk like I'm old enough to be your father."

"Well, you do treat me like a child sometimes."

"No I don't," he argued.

"Yes, you do. You tell me what to do and how and when."

"Sometimes you act like a child."

"No, I don't," she disagreed.

"Yes, you do."

"Then we're even," she ended the argument.

His smile flipped her heart. "I have to go in early tomorrow. Can you be ready by 6:30 or do you want to take the L?"

"I'll ride with you. Why do you have to go early?"

"To see if I can catch another Leprechaun in my shower," he teased.

"What, one isn't enough for you?"

"More than enough!" His eyes caressed her. "I have a meeting. I'm going to bed. I suggest you... umm... go whenever you like."

"Yes, Dad," Brianna said. John shook his head before heading for his room.

Brianna watched him go, then turned back to the lake view. She definitely did not think of him as a father. Damn! Why did he have to be her boss? She sighed. *I do not need a man running my life.*

* * * *

John leaned back in his chair and put his feet up on his desk, running a pencil between his fingers. He fixed his gaze on the lake beyond the window. He'd only known Brianna a short time yet he had a feeling his life was about to change drastically.

He had spent the last twelve years of his life making this company what is but at what cost? Thirty-seven years old and this is all I have to show for it, he thought. This business. He missed the early days when he only had a handful of employees and he knew them all by name. He worked side by side with them. Now, nearly a hundred people worked for him and he didn't know half of their names. He missed writing ad copy, coming up with catchy slogans and sketching ideas.

He sat up and picked up his phone, "Mrs. Wilson, would you come in here, please."

Mrs. Wilson came in and sat on the edge of the chair he had indicated.

"Your name is Sandy, right?"

"Yes."

"Would you mind if I called you that?"

"No, sir." Mrs. Wilson shook her head, clearly perplexed.

John smiled, "It's been pointed out to me that it's a little 'stuffy' around here. Would you agree with that?"

"Stuffy? It's a pleasant working environment, a little formal, perhaps," she said, hesitantly.

"Formal, certainly sounds better than stuffy," he mused. "Do you think it is formal to the point of stifling creativity?"

"I wouldn't say that. A company this size needs a certain amount of formality."

"It needs structure but I'm not sure about the formality. That's all, Sandy. Thanks."

"Yes, sir."

"One more thing, you can drop the 'sir.' It makes me feel old," he smiled.

"Yes, s… Mr. Sharp." She went back to her desk.

That felt good. What else could he do? He picked up the phone again.

"Sandy, would you send for Brianna Ryan in graphics, please?"

While he waited for Brianna, he took off his jacket and hung it on the back of his chair, he thought a second, pulled off his tie, unbuttoned a couple of buttons at the neck and rolled back his sleeves. He was tapping a pencil when she came in.

He stood up, spread his arms and turned around, showing off his casual appearance.

"What do you think?"

Brianna grinned. "It's a start. Is this what you called me in here for?"

"Yes, and I've been thinking about how you said it was 'stuffy' here. What do you think we could do to un-stuffy it?"

"You're kidding, right?"

"No, I'm completely serious. Work shouldn't be all grind, there should be some fun elements. I think it would stimulate creativity. I'm sure you have some ideas. Let me have them."

"Where do I start? I've been thinking it would be a good idea to have an employee support group, a couple of employees from each department where we could go to discuss any problems and concerns we have about our jobs. The group could meet once a month and bring concerns to management."

"That's a great idea," he said. "I thought about doing a survey, asking about likes and dislikes, changes they would like to see, that sort of thing."

"That would be good. Something I think you, personally, could do is visit the departments once in awhile. Just walk around, talk to people, and get to know your employees. It would make you more approachable. It would be good if all the suits did it once in a while," Brianna said.

"Suits?" John wasn't up on office slang.

"Executives. The ones that wear suits," Brianna informed him.

"Oh. I could do that. I'll mention it to the other 'suits' at Monday's staff meeting. Anything else we could implement immediately?"

"We could put up a notice about a company picnic, ask for volunteers to help plan it. It could be simple, a cookout in a park, a few games and prizes. It would bring people together from different departments and it would be a lot of fun."

"I like it. I'll leave the details up to you. Stay and help me work out the survey. I'd like to get that out as soon as possible. I'll clear it with Miss Davis."

They had been working on the survey for nearly an hour when Kaitlyn walked in unannounced. Brianna sat at John's desk, inputting their ideas on the computer. John was leaning over her. Kaitlyn noticed John's open shirt.

"Well, isn't this cozy. It seems you're here every time I come in. What's going on this time?" Her presence seemed to drop the temperature in the room by at least ten degrees.

"We're working on a special project, Kaitlyn." John said.

"I need to talk to you."

"Okay. What?"

"Alone, if you don't mind." Kaitlyn said.

"We can work on this later, Bree. It's your lunch break, isn't it?"

Kaitlyn watched Brianna until the door closed behind her.

"Bree?" She raised a brow. "Every time I need to talk to you she's here," Kaitlyn said. "You've got your jacket and tie off, your shirt unbuttoned. This is not like you."

"I felt stuffy." John said.

"Stuffy? Couldn't you just turn up the air-conditioning? What is this special project you're working on?"

"I'll tell you about it when we get more of the details worked out. What did you want to see me about?"

143

"There's something different about you and I'm not sure I like it," Kaitlyn said. "You're half undressed with that redheaded twit in here, working on projects I know nothing about. This is a place of business not a social club."

"I am not 'half undressed' and Brianna is not a twit. She's very bright. I'm well aware that this is a place of business. It is, after all, *my* business. Is there a law that says a business has to be drab?" John met her gaze, "What did you want to see me about?"

"Take me to lunch and we'll discuss it."

"All right, Kaitlyn. Let's go." John walked toward the door.

"Aren't you going to put on your tie and jacket?" Kaitlyn asked.

"No. I'm not."

"You can't get into the Voltaire without them," Kaitlyn said, mentioning her favorite, expensive French restaurant.

"We're not going to the Voltaire." John said.

Kaitlyn glared at him for a moment before she turned and stalked out ahead of him. John smiled and followed her out.

"We're going to lunch, Sandy," he said to his secretary.

"Yes, s.., okay."

"Sandy? Since when do you address your secretary as Sandy?" Kaitlyn asked when the elevator door closed.

"Since today," John said. Kaitlyn cocked an eyebrow but kept silent.

They reached the lobby and Kaitlyn turned toward the parking garage, John went to the front door.

"Aren't we taking your car?"

"We can walk. It's not far."

"I can't walk in these shoes." Kaitlyn held out a foot clad in an expensive, high-heeled, pointy-toed shoe.

"If you can't walk in them, why do you wear them?" She shot him an annoyed look. "It's less than a block away. I want to try that new Italian place on the corner," John said.

Kaitlyn walked stiffly and silently beside him. When they reached the restaurant, John held the door for her. The hostess approached them.

"Table for two?" she asked. Kaitlyn nodded. "Would you like an inside table or one on the patio?"

"Inside." Kaitlyn said.

At the same time, John said, "The patio, please." Kaitlyn glared at him. "It's a lovely, spring day. The air will do you good."

Kaitlyn followed the girl. "Something in the shade," she demanded.

"Could I get you something to drink?" the hostess asked, handing them menus.

"Do you have a wine list?" Kaitlyn asked.

"I'll just have ice tea, please and bring the lady a glass of Merlot."

"A glass of Merlot? Just 'Merlot?' How do you know it's a good Merlot without seeing the wine list?" Kaitlyn questioned when the hostess left.

"It will be fine, Kaitlyn. Quit being such a snob."

"I am not a snob. I just know what I like and don't like and, lately, I don't like your attitude."

"Oh, for Pete's sake, Kaitlyn, loosen up. Don't you ever want to have fun, let go and enjoy yourself?"

"What has gotten into you, John?"

"Nothing's 'gotten into me.' I just decided 'all work and no play makes Johnny a dull boy.'"

"I think that's 'makes Jack a dull boy,' not Johnny."

"What was so important that you wanted to talk about?" John said.

The waitress came to take their orders.

"I'll have the grilled chicken salad, no dressing just a lemon on the side and no onions." Kaitlyn ordered. "And, another glass of this wine." She indicated the nearly empty glass with distaste.

"What do you recommend?" John asked.

"My favorite is the lobster stuffed ravioli with shrimp sauce, served over linguine."

"That sounds excellent. And, I'll have the spicy Italian dressing on my salad. Thank you."

"Daddy's throwing a sixtieth birthday party for himself at the club Saturday. I want you to come."

John pulled his phone from his pocket.

"Sorry, Kaitlyn. I already have plans Saturday."

Kaitlyn glared at him for a moment over her wine glass.

John listened to roughly a quarter of what Kaitlyn said during the meal. He vaguely heard the words, party, shopping, masseuse and stylist before he tuned her out completely.

He watched people walking by on the busy sidewalk. A young family caught his attention.

They were laughing at something the little redheaded girl said. They looked happy.

"John, have you heard a word I've said?"

"Hmm? Oh, sorry, Kaitlyn. My thoughts wandered off, I guess."

"What's more important than me?" Kaitlyn said.

"I'm sure nothing is more important than you, Kaitlyn," John said silkily, as the waitress handed him the check.

She turned and stomped through the restaurant.

CHAPTER ELEVEN

Saturday morning, Brianna sat at the breakfast bar sipping tea while studying the transit schedule. She glanced up as John entered the room, but quickly returned to the schedule. It wasn't fair for a man to look that good when he was all hot and sweaty from a workout.

"So, today's the big day." John wiped his face on a corner of the towel around his neck.

Brianna nodded without taking her eyes off the paper. John poured a glass of orange juice and took a large sip.

"Give me thirty minutes to shower and we can go."

"You're going? That really isn't necessary. I'm perfectly capable of finding my own apartment."

149

"I'm sure you are." John looked down and shrugged his shoulders. "but, I have a list, too, and it will be a lot easier in a car than riding the "L.""

"Like I can afford anything on your list," Brianna said.

"You'd be surprised. I kept your budget in mind."

"Ha!" Brianna slid off the barstool.

"I am taking you. It'll be fun. Get dressed."

"You are, without a doubt, one of the bossiest men I know." She stomped from the room.

"Promise you'll wait for me." John called after her.

"Okay but you have to promise to keep quiet or you'll be waitin' in the car," she answered.

* * * *

"Where's your car?" Brianna asked, looking around for the Mercedes.

"Right here," John said, opening the door of a bright red, BMW convertible.

Brianna's jaw dropped.

"Wha'…where…?"

"I rented it this morning just for the fun of it and the look on your face is worth every penny.

Where should we start?" John asked, starting the car.

"It's my apartment so we'll start with my list." Brianna declared, settling into the creamy leather upholstery. "Most of them are west of the loop near the Kennedy-Eisenhower exchange."

Brianna watched John as he drove along the lakeshore. He was dressed casually in jeans and a light blue polo shirt. *He could make a potato sack look gorgeous.* She loved the way the wind dared to ruffle his hair. She folded her hands tightly in her lap to keep her fingers from running through it. John glanced her way and smiled.

"If you'd have told me Monday that I would be doing this, I would have called you crazy."

"But you're enjoying it. I can tell."

"Immensely," John said as he downshifted around a corner, the back of his hand accidentally brushing her bare thigh, causing her to inhale sharply. Curse this small car, I should've worn jeans, Brianna thought, moving her leg.

"I think I like this car. I may have to buy one," he said, grinning at her. He pulled up to the curb near a run-down building, the first address on Brianna's list.

"This doesn't look too bad," Brianna said, as she got out of the car.

She could tell that John was not favorably impressed but he kept silent as she knocked on the manager's door. The sounds of a blaring television and noisy children were heard when a middle-aged woman with a cigarette dangling from the corner of her mouth opened the door a crack.

"Who's there?" the woman said.

"We're here to see the apartment you have for rent," John said.

"Yeah, just a minute," She closed the door, screamed at the kids, slid the chain lock off and shuffled into the dim hallway. The heavyset woman with straggly, mouse-brown hair, wore tight spandex leggings and a faded, over-sized T-shirt; she had obviously forgotten a bra.

"'Sup' here," she said, cigarette still dangling.

She led them two flights up a narrow staircase marred by graffiti and dirty hand prints and inserted the key into a door marked '3C.'

They walked into a narrow hall that lead to a large room with three grimy windows offering a view of the next building. There was a door on either side of the little hallway.

"Bathroom," said the woman indicating the door on the left. "Closet." She pointed to the other one.

They entered the large room. A small refrigerator, sink and stove sat along part of one wall with sagging selves above them.

"Where's the bedroom?" Brianna asked when she couldn't locate another door.

"Ain't, no bedroom. Jist this here bed." She grabbed a handle and the bed crashed to the floor sending up a cloud of dust from the cracked linoleum floor. Brianna jumped back to protect her toes and gasped when she saw the mattress. It looked like a relic from the St. Valentine's Day Massacre.

John opened the refrigerator and immediately slammed it shut, taking a step back. He gave Brianna a look of disgust and shook his head. Brianna looked into the dingy, windowless bathroom; it had all the required equipment, along with grungy tile and a stained tub but no shower. She'd seen enough.

"I was hoping for a one bedroom but I'll let you know," Brianna said to the woman. "Thank you."

They walked to the car.

"That was appalling. There was moldy food in the refrigerator," John said as they pulled away from the curb.

"Did you see that mattress? That's going to give me nightmares for a week!" Brianna shuddered. "The bathroom was awful, too. I was afraid something furry was going to crawl out of the corner. On the bright side, they can only get better from here."

"Ah, yes. Brianna, the eternal optimist. Let us hope."

The second and third were only slightly better. The fourth was most likely worse. Three men were smoking on the front steps. John wouldn't even stop for that one. They parked in the lot next to the fifth one and got out.

"This is the last one on my list," Brianna said, her shoulders drooping. "It looks promising."

"It is a newer building. And, there's a bus stop on the corner," John said, determined to keep an open mind as they walked up the steps to the front door. The sign on the manager's office read, 'Come In.' A bell jingled as they opened the door and a teen-aged boy appeared from a back room dressed in baggy jeans with holes in the knees and a black T-shirt depicting a punk rock band on the front. He had a ring in his nose connected to a looped chain dangling from one eyebrow. His black hair was stiffly spiked.

"You here about the apartment?" he asked, looking Brianna up and down.

"Yes," Brianna said, as John tried to steer her out of the room.

"No," John gave Brianna a stern look.

"We might as well look since we're here." Brianna pulled from his grasp. "It's the best looking building we've seen. You can wait in the car."

"Not on your life!" John said. "Are you the manager?"

"Nope, my mom is but she works mornings."

"Do you have a name?"

"Dustin," he answered John. "But you can call me 'Dusty,'" he winked at Brianna. He led them to a short stairway. "It's called a 'garden level' unit," he announced.

John followed them down the stairs to the basement apartment.

They entered a small living room where the window provided a stunning view of people's feet as they walked by.

"Lovely view," John said. Brianna shot him a warning look.

Dustin showed her the windowless kitchen that was adequate and clean compared to others they had seen this morning.

"It's too dark," John commented.

They were led to the small bedroom where the underside of cars were visible in the rear parking lot.

"This room would barely fit a bed."

"One more word and you're going to the car!" Brianna said.

There was a tiny bathroom with a tiny metal shower stall in the corner.

"That shower isn't big enough for an adult!" John said. Brianna elbowed his ribs.

"Man, your dad sure is picky," Dusty said to Brianna.

Brianna looked at John, barely able to contain her laughter, a job made harder by the red line creeping up his neck.

"I am not her father," John said through clenched teeth.

Brianna was sure it was only a matter of time before steam burst from John's ears and the top of his head blew off. She quickly steered him out of the apartment before he exploded.

"I'll let you know," she said to Dusty over her shoulder.

Brianna lost it as soon as she got in the car. Tears were streaming down her face by the time John started the engine.

"It's not funny. I am not old enough to be your father!"

Brianna, doubled over hugging her sides, could only shake her head.

"I'm sorry, but that was definitely funny."

"From your view point apparently. Not from mine."

"Oh, come on. He was just a kid and you *were* acting like a father, *again*."

"He may be just a kid but he looked at you like you were a piece of candy."

"He was not," Brianna said. "It is at the top of my price range so they're not likely to get much better. It wasn't that bad."

"Compared to the others we've seen but that's not saying much. There is no way on God's green earth that I would let you live there."

"I'm starved," Brianna said, allowing the 'let you' to slide, for now. "There's a pizza place just around the corner. It's the best pizza in the city."

"You *know* this neighborhood?" John asked.

"I lived with my aunt just a few blocks over near St. Patrick's Church." She pointed to the left.

John was still steaming when they entered the pizzeria. A man tossed dough in the corner kitchen area of the dimly lit room. The spicy aroma coming from the hot brick ovens along the wall made Brianna's mouth water. A jukebox played a popular song and several people ate at tables covered with red-checkered cloths. They chose a corner one. A wax-covered wine bottle in the center held a candle stub.

Brianna lightly punched John's shoulder, "Come on, cheer up. I don't think of you as my father, even if you do act like it sometimes. He was a kid, to him anyone over thirty is old."

The waiter took their order and returned with large glasses of soda.

"Tell me about your family. You mentioned brothers the other night."

"Yeah, there are four of them. I'm the baby by several years."

John unwrapped the straws and placed one in each glass.

"That's a lot of boys to put up with."

"Tell me about it. A testosterone nightmare."

John laughed. "So, where did you grow up – I know you're from Ireland."

"I grew up in a centuries old stone house on a small sheep farm in County Galway near Dunmore until I got sent to the states." Her eyes clouded.

He nodded, "Go on."

"At fourteen, I was quite rebellious. Papa and the boys didn't know what to do with me after Mum took sick." She looked up and saw a flicker of sympathy in John's eyes. "I'd sneak out my window at night and meet friends. One night, Sean — he's the youngest — caught me making out with a neighbor boy. He was older and had a bad reputation. Maybe that's why I liked him." Brianna chuckled. "Anyway, Sean told Michael — my oldest brother — who told Papa. He sent me to bed and nailed my window shut—" John's jaw dropped. She tilted her head and gave him a lopsided smile. "—the "men" had a discussion that decided my fate. I was shipped off to Chicago to live with my dad's older sister and her husband."

"That must have been hard on you." John briefly touched her hand.

"Yeah, well, life isn't always easy. Aunt Tillie was a timid little woman and Uncle Bruce was a real tyrant. He didn't want to be bothered with me. I think the only reason he agreed to my coming to live with them was the money Papa sent every month. Uncle Bruce's job as a janitor at the high school didn't pay a whole lot. 'I have to put up with hooligans all day, I'll not be puttin' up with one in me own house,' he said." She mimicked his gruff Irish brogue. "He was a big, burly Irishman. Scared the daylights out of me, he did. He died about a year after I arrived."

"What happened?" John asked as the waiter set their drinks on the table.

"Heart attack. One minute he was ranting at poor Aunt Tillie about hard potatoes in the stew– Aunt Till wasn't a very good cook. Uncle Bruce yelled a lot about that– " She paused to take a sip of her Coke. "– and the next minute he was face down in his bowl, splat!" She slapped the table with her palm.

John inhaled a mouthful of his drink and grabbed for a napkin as his face turned red. Brianna jumped up and pounded him on the back.

"I'm okay. I'm fine," John sputtered through the napkin he held over his mouth.

Brianna returned to her seat but kept a worried eye on John as he wiped the corners of his eyes and regained his composure.

"Go on." His voice was still raspy.

"Well, Aunt Tillie was getting old and her health wasn't so good. Besides, she didn't know how to do much of anything so I went to work at the local pub."

"A pub? At your age?"

"The owner was a friend of the family. I washed dishes and cleaned up."

"Not much of a life for a kid."

"It wasn't so bad, really." Brianna shrugged her shoulders. "A little work never hurt anyone." The waiter set the pizza on their table. "Ahh, saved by the pizza."

John put a slice on his plate and reached for a knife and fork but Brianna covered his hand.

"You can't eat pizza with a fork," she admonished, grabbing a piece and biting into it. "You have to eat it with your fingers to appreciate the full flavor." She licked a bit of sauce from the corner of her mouth.

John gulped, picked up his slice and bit into it.

"Delicious," he said.

* * * *

"Now, it's time for my picks," John said as they got into the car.

"This ought to be good. What are the chances of there being anything I can afford on that list?"

"You'll see. I kept your pocketbook in mind."

Brianna was skeptical but humored him.

John headed northeast and took the lakeshore drive.

"There's nothing in Lincoln Park that I can afford," Brianna said when John turned into the parking lot of a complex.

"There might be."

They looked at two that had lake views, and another one a block from the beach. All were very modern, very cold and very expensive. John turned onto a tree-lined boulevard about two blocks from the lake. He stopped in front of a pretty English Tudor style house. It was small compared to the other houses on the block but still quite large by her standards.

"I can't afford anything like this," she said.

"I'm not showing you the whole house," John said. "According to the paper, there is a small apartment over the garage. It's worth looking at and might be affordable."

"Yeah, like all the others you found." Brianna followed him up the curved walk to the front door. John lifted the brass knocker.

A tall woman with silver streaked dark hair answered the door.

"Hello. Are you the young man that called about the apartment?" Brianna knew that made his day.

"Yes. I'm John Sharp and this is my friend, Brianna Ryan. She's the one interested in the apartment," John said. Brianna shook the offered hand.

"I'm Mrs. Whitley. Please come in." The interior was wonderfully cool and tastefully decorated. Mrs. Whitley led them through the living and dining rooms to the kitchen. "The apartment is back here, above the garage."

They walked across the flagstone patio, bordered by a large shady lawn, to the garage. She unlocked a door on the side revealing a stairway to the upper floor.

At the top of the stairs there was a large living-dining room with windows on two sides and a breakfast bar at one end, dividing the galley kitchen from the main room. In the back was a bedroom that looked out on the lawn, and a bathroom. It had an old claw-foot tub that Brianna fell in love with.

"It's a lovely apartment, Mrs. Whitley. How much is the rent?"

Mrs. Whitley named a price that was well within Brianna's budget.

"Excuse me?" Brianna was sure she had misunderstood. "I'm not sure I heard you right."

Mrs. Whitley repeated the figure. Brianna looked at John.

"Could I see you outside for a minute?" she said to John.

"What? You don't like it?" John asked, when they were out of Mrs. Whitley's range.

"I love it," Brianna said, "but how can she rent it so cheap? I feel like I would be taking advantage of her."

"Mrs. Whitley," John called to the woman. "Brianna wants to know why you are renting this so cheap." Brianna slapped his arm, John grinned. "Is there something wrong with the apartment that we should know about?"

Mrs. Whitley came into the room. "There's nothing wrong with it, young man."

"I'm so sorry, Mrs. Whitley," Brianna said, glaring at John.

"It's all right, dear. Men can be maddening sometimes, can't they?" she gave John a stern look and patted Brianna's arm. "Pay no attention to him. My husband died a few years ago and I don't need the money. This was the servant's quarter's years ago. My nephew suggested I fix it up and rent it out just to have someone near," she fixed John with another glare.

"How soon could I move in?" Brianna asked.

"There's still some plumbing and electrical work to finish up. I'm sure it will be ready by the end of the month."

"That's wonderful," Brianna said, barely able to contain her excitement.

They followed Mrs. Whitley back to her house. Brianna signed a lease and John offered to pay a deposit but Mrs. Whitley insisted it wasn't necessary.

Brianna danced backward all the way to the car, afraid if she took her eyes off her garage it would disappear. She couldn't believe her luck. A beautiful apartment in a beautiful neighborhood and it was affordable. She'd surely died and gone to heaven.

"Let's celebrate," John said as he turned onto North Shore Drive. "We'll go home, change and go somewhere nice for dinner."

"I know a fun place and we wouldn't have to change clothes," Brianna said. "It's near the place we ate lunch, though." John looked doubtful. "Really, you'll love it. Irish food, Irish beer, and Irish music."

"If you say so," John said as he turned the car around.

"I do."

When they entered Paddy's Pub, Brianna waved at the stout, redheaded bartender.

"Evenin' Breeze. Haven't seen you in a while," he said.

"Hey, Paddy. Some of us gotta work for a livin' ya know," Brianna said. "This is my friend, John,"

"John, pleased to meet ya," Paddy shook John's hand. "A friend of Breeze's is a friend of Paddy's. What can I git ya?"

"A couple of pints of Guinness, Paddy." Brianna led the way to a booth in the corner, greeting several more people on the way.

"You seem to know a lot of people here," John said.

"I told you, I used to live around here. This is where I worked."

Paddy set the foamy mugs of ale on the table. "You be wantin' t' eat? Mary's brewin' a pot o' her famous stew."

"Not just yet, Paddy, thanks." Brianna said. "Come on," she said grabbing John's hand. "Bring your beer."

John grabbed his beer with his free hand while Brianna pulled him to the piano where a short man in a bowler hat, green vest and a red plaid bow-tie had just sat down to play. He placed a stein on top of the piano for tips.

"Any requests?" he shouted.

Several people called out various tunes, mostly Irish. He began with "When Irish Eyes Are Smiling." Everyone joined in, singing loudly.

"This is your song," John said, leaning close to Brianna's ear. He raised his mug to hers and smiled into the emerald green depths of her Irish eyes.

Brianna could feel the heat rising in her cheeks. She turned and took a paper from the top of the piano. "Here," she said, handing it to John, "the words to most of the songs. You'll need them later. Some of the songs are not well known." She flashed a mischievous grin.

One hour later, they sat at their table. "Maybe we should eat something." John said. "What do you suggest?"

"We could try Mary's Irish stew, it's very good or they have wonderful corned beef on rye. Or... how about both? One of each and we'll share."

Brianna hailed the waitress. John watched the sway of her hips as she approached the table. Brianna nudged him with her foot.

"Hi, Erin. We're ready to order," Brianna ordered for them. "This is Paddy's daughter. Erin, this is John."

"A pleasure, Erin," John said. His gaze lingered on the expanse of cleavage displayed when Erin leaned over to pick up the empty mugs and replace them with full ones. Brianna nudged him harder.

"She's married," Brianna said, when Erin had left.

"Damn!" John said, quickly moving his leg. Brianna kicked his chair and winced. She glared at him.

"Not only is she married, she has two kids."

John released an exaggerated sigh of disappointment. Brianna smacked him with her napkin.

Erin returned and set a large, steaming bowl of stew in front of them along with a sandwich stacked high with corned beef and Swiss cheese.

"That's a small bowl?" John asked. "It's a wonder everyone doesn't weigh 300 pounds around here." He picked up a sandwich half and attempted to smash it thin enough to fit his mouth.

"We'll work it off later," Brianna said. John gave her a questioning look. "I always get a little home sick when I come here." She forked a cube of meat from the stew and put it into her mouth.

When they had finished eating, Brianna got up and grabbed John's hand.

"I'm too full to move," he said in protest, leaning back and rubbing his stomach.

She pulled him up and led him back to the piano where the music had been steadily getting faster and louder. A fiddler had joined in. Several people were dancing an Irish line dance.

"I can't understand the words," John said, raising his voice above the clamor.

"That's probably for the best," Brianna replied with a smile. She showed him how to do the dance. He caught on quickly and soon kept up with the others with only minor miss-steps.

After several songs, they sat down to catch their breath and quench their parched throats. Brianna barely had time to set her mug down when a local patron seized her hand and pulled her back to the dance floor for an old-fashioned Irish jig.

John watched, fascinated by the lively steps as they increased their pace to keep up with the music. Brianna finally collapsed in her partner's arms, exhausted but exhilarated. He escorted her back to the table.

"This here's the best little jigger this side of the Atlantic," he declared. "You take real good care o' her."

John nodded, keeping his eyes on Brianna's flushed face and sparkling eyes.

"Are you having a good time?" she asked John.

"Incredible," he answered. "Hey, they're playing your song again." He pulled a reluctant Brianna to her feet.

"You can't be serious. My feet are killing me and I can barely breathe."

"Come on. It's slow and you can lean on me."

John turned her into his arms. He signaled the musicians to slow the tempo a bit more.

Brianna could feel the beating of his heart beneath her cheek as she relied on him to keep her upright. Her left hand curved around his neck as he tightened his hold on her waist. As the song ended, he twirled her around and caught her to his side. He grasped her waist and lifted her off her feet, letting her slide down his body as the little band played the opening cords of 'Danny Boy.'

"Let's go. This is the last song and it always makes me cry," Brianna said.

"All ready?" John glanced at his watch, surprised to see that it was past two in the morning.

Brianna hummed 'When Irish Eyes Are Smiling' all the way home. John kept a steadying arm around the sleepy girl until they reached her bedroom door. He grasped her shoulders and kissed the top of her head.

"Thanks for a delightful evening, my little Irish rose," he caressed her cheek with the back of his hand before gently pushing her into her room. She gave him a dreamy smile and closed the door. John waited a moment before walking down the hall to his room.

CHAPTER TWELVE

Brianna woke with a smile, humming "Oh, What a Beautiful Morning." In the shower she sang an array of Irish tunes. She finished the last chorus of "My Wild Irish Rose" as she entered the kitchen, surprised and disappointed, to find it empty.

She filled her teapot and set it on the stove and made a cup of coffee for John. She sat at the bar with her bowl of cereal when John wandered in looking wonderfully disheveled. He went straight for the coffee.

"Good morning," Brianna chirped.

"Hm," he replied, holding up a hand. "Don't talk until I've had some caffeine."

"Rough night?" Brianna lowered her head to hide a smile.

He leaned against the counter, closed his eyes and gulped the steaming liquid.

After finishing her Cheerios in silence, she brewed a cup of tea for herself and another cup of coffee for John.

"Ahh, I feel almost human," he said as he drained his second cup. "I never sleep this late. It's your fault, keeping me out until the wee hours dancing like a young pup. This morning I feel old enough to be your father."

"Aww. You poor old man. You'll feel better after a nice hot bath. Should I run one for you?" Brianna teased.

"Feeling a bit cheeky this morning, aren't we?"

"I feel wonderful. I have a new apartment that I love and, even better, that I can afford."

"Tired of living with me?"

"No, not at all, but I'll bet you'll be glad to get rid of me."

John gazed at her intently before pushing away from the counter. "I'm going to take a shower."

When he returned, Brianna set a piece of toast and another cup of coffee in front of him. "What are your plans for the weekend?"

"Just a little R and R." He picked up his cup. "What are you doing?"

"I'm going to the beach with Carly. It's Rob's weekend to work. Why don't you ask Ms. Schuster out?"

"Kaitlyn?" John set his cup down and looked at her. "Why would I do that?"

"Because she likes you and you have a lot in common and you need some fun in your life." She ticked off the reasons on her fingers.

"Oh, I do, do I? And, what makes you think she likes me?"

"I've heard talk at work."

"You mean gossip." He looked at her over the rim of his mug.

"Call it what you want. The fact is she's a ladder climber," Brianna declared smugly.

"A what?" John asked.

"A ladder climber. You know, someone who wants to better herself and be successful." Brianna said, adding naively, "According to the girls, she knows the fast track up the corporate ladder."

John spewed coffee, set the cup down and laughed. "Do you have any idea what that means?"

"It's a good thing, isn't it? Wanting to better yourself." Brianna bit her lip.

John grinned before explaining. "It means sleeping your way to the top"

Brianna's jaw dropped and she felt the heat rising in her cheeks until she was sure her face matched her hair. She stared at him wide-eyed.

John picked up his cup and took a sip. He seemed to be enjoying her embarrassment. He set the cup down. "They think she's sleeping with *me*?"

"Oh, no!" Brianna shook her head. "They just think she would like to— go out with you, not sleep with you, I'm sure." She wished she could just fade into the woodwork.

John shook his head and left the room.

* * * *

A couple of hours later, she met Carly at North Avenue Beach.

"Let's grab a sandwich at the Castaways," Carly said naming the popular restaurant above the shops at the park. "Did you find an apartment? I tried calling you a couple of times last night."

"We got in very late," Brianna said. "I found the most wonderful place in Lincoln Park. A widow renovated a servant's quarters above her garage. It's charming and so is she. It's as if she decorated it with me in mind. I love everything about it. I can't wait to move in."

"The shar—boss getting on your nerves, is he?"

"No, he's been really great," Brianna said. "It's just that I need my own place. I can't stay there forever."

"Do I detect a hint of regret?" Carly asked.

"No... Yes... Maybe. I don't know, Carly. He's different when he's away from work. He rented a red convertible yesterday just for me. We had such a good time looking at apartments, even the awful ones. We went to Paddy's Pub last night and danced until early morning."

"Where is he today?"

"At home. I told him he should take Ms. Schuster out."

"You did *what?*" She noticed Brianna's dismal expression. "You're falling in love with him aren't you?"

"I...don't...I think... maybe. Yes," she finally admitted to Carly, and herself. "But it wouldn't work. We're too different. It could never work."

"You don't know that. It could work. It certainly sounds like he's interested in you."

"Interested maybe, but not in love. I'm a novelty to him. He likes smart, sophisticated, beautiful women. I'm different. I amuse him. He may be interested but he'll never buy, the novelty would soon wear off. Where would that leave me? Broken-hearted, that's where. I don't think I'd get over this one easily. No, it's better this way."

"Better for whom? You underestimate yourself, Bree. You're smart, attractive, charming, funny and passionate. Sophistication never kept any man warm at night."

They finished lunch and headed for the beach. Carly squeezed her shoulder. "Let's find a volleyball game." Brianna shook her head. "Come on. It'll be good for you, work off some of that pent up– frustration!"

* * * *

When she got home there was a note from John saying he had gone to play golf and would be eating at the club. He didn't say with whom.

Certain that he would not be back for hours; Brianna made use of his large tub again. She had just finished soaking away the aches of hours of activity in the sun and wrapped herself in a bath sheet when she heard John in the bedroom.

"You're home early," she called through the adjoining door, warning him of her presence.

"Are you about done in there? I need a shower."

"I was just coming out," she answered, opening the door. *Oh, Lord,* she thought, wishing he would put his shirt back on so her heart could beat normally. *Exhaust myself with hours of frustration relieving activity and now I'm right back where I started.*

John took one look at her and exclaimed, "Good Lord! Your skin is as red as your hair. We need to put something on that before it blisters."

He guided her back into his bathroom. Pulling a bottle of Aloe Vera out of the cabinet, he motioned for her to turn around. The gel felt cool on her hot skin as he gently smoothed it across her back and shoulders.

Brianna asked. "Who did you play golf with?"

"Dr. Anderson." He turned her around to apply gel to her nose and cheeks.

Happy that he didn't say 'Kaitlyn,' she gave a sigh of relief.

"Feels better, doesn't it?"

Brianna nodded. *If he only knew how good.* She sighed again.

When he started to put some gel on her chest, she took the bottle from him.

"I can manage the rest," she said, leaving him to take his shower.

* * * *

She dressed and wandered out to the balcony. John joined her within a few minutes.

His eyes locked on her mouth. Brianna ran her tongue over her lower lip as her heart did a back flip and landed in her stomach. He briefly raised his eyes to hers before turning away. She took a deep breath.

"I—" Her voice squeaked. She cleared her throat. "I really think you should ask Kaitlyn out." *I am crazy.*

John turned to face her, folding his arms across his chest and leaning against the balustrade.

"You're like a dog with a bone. Just let it go. I usually make it a point not to get involved with people I work with."

Brianna flicked her gaze to the stars, released a heavy sigh and took a step toward him.

"But she likes you." She spread her arms, palms up.

John's mouth twitched. "You like me. Maybe I should ask you out."

Brianna stepped back. "I'm serious. You're not getting any younger and you're too nice and good-looking to spend the rest of your life alone." Why did her tongue never fail her when she needed it too. One of the great mysteries of the Universe.

"So you think I'm nice and good-looking but too old. Too old for what? Romance? Love?" His eyes locked with hers. "You?"

Brianna's eyes widened. She took another step back.

"That's not what I meant and you know it." She frowned at him and put her hands on her hips.

John chuckled, "Oh. You meant I should find someone before I lose my good looks and become a lonely, grouchy old man."

She glared at him.

"Now you're just poking fun at me."

She spun on her heel intent on leaving the terrace but John caught her arm halting her in mid-stride.

"I'm sorry," he said.

Brianna looked at the hand on her arm spreading warmth. She suppressed the desire to cover it with her own, to lace her fingers with his. She squeezed her eyes and inhaled shakily.

180

"Apology accepted." Facing him, she said, "I still think you should ask Ms. Schuster out." John groaned but Brianna wouldn't be swayed. "It's obvious she likes you."

"Subtlety is not one of her strong points. Are you sure it's me or a promotion she wants?"

His gaze fastened on her mouth again. Brianna contemplated his for a moment until they both looked away. She knew she should retreat to the safety of her room but her Irish heritage won out. She stubbornly—foolishly—stood her ground.

"Okay." John brought his eyes back to hers. "I'll ask her out but only if we make it a double date."

"I don't think—I mean, I don't know any—that is not what I had in mind."

"That's the deal. And I know the perfect guy for you."

"I can get my own date, thank you." Brianna narrowed her eyes and set her jaw.

"You picked my date so I get to pick yours. Dinner Saturday night good for you?" The amused glint in his eyes had Brianna seething.

"Fine," she said, through clenched teeth before leaving the terrace. The sound of John's chuckle followed her through the living room.

* * * *

Despite the physical exhaustion, Brianna did not sleep well. Plagued by senseless dreams and the stinging sunburn, she gave up at dawn and climbed out of bed. She went into the kitchen and poured a glass of juice before wandering out to the terrace.

The deep pink of dawn gave way to lighter pinks, streaked with orange, as the sun began its journey across the sky. It encountered no problems, no setbacks, no confusion along its path. It rose and set every day, laughing in the face of storms. Why couldn't her life be that simple? Get up, go to work, come home, go to bed, no turmoil, no uncertainty, no misunderstandings... no emotion, no passion, no life. Well, maybe she didn't want her life to be that simple but did it have to be completely bewildering? Couldn't she just find the right man? The problem was she had found her Mr. Right; she just wasn't his Ms. Right!

"And that's a fact," she said, draining her juice.

"What's a fact?" the deep voice startled her. The glass slipped from her grasp, shattering on the tiled floor.

"I didn't hear you come out. Ouch!" she said as she stepped on a large shard of the broken glass. She raised her foot to remove the glass.

John saw the blood trickle from the cut in her foot and wasted no time scooping her up and carrying her toward his bathroom. Brianna protested briefly but looped her arm around his neck and enjoyed the ride. *Too bad it's such a short distance*, she thought, mentally shaking herself. *I really need to get a better grip on my thoughts.*

John set her on the counter. "Put your foot in the sink," he commanded.

Brianna swung around and complied while he gathered supplies from the cabinet. She bit her lip as he ran water over the wound.

"There isn't any glass in there," he said after gently probing and drying the area. Brianna pulled her foot back and sucked in a breath.

"I'm sorry. I didn't mean to hurt you."

Brianna shook her head. Pain is not the word she would use to describe the sensation running up her leg.

He applied antiseptic and a bandage. "There you go, good as new."

She swung her legs off the counter but John prevented her from jumping down by placing his hands on either side of her hips. She could feel the warmth of his hands through her thin pajama pants, warmth that quickly spread throughout her body. He searched her face as his head lowered, slowly, until his cell phone rang in the bedroom. He dropped his head, took a deep breath and straightened. His eyes held a hint of regret before he went to answer it. Brianna slid off the counter and retreated to her room.

A few minutes later John stopped at her open door. "I'm going over to Kaitlyn's. She can't get a hold of her building super and there seems to be a problem with her AC. I'll be back soon."

Not if Kaitlyn has her way .

She stood under the shower letting the cold spray cool her heated body. *Funny, I've heard of a man taking a cold shower but never a woman. If the phone hadn't rung–* Her cheeks burned despite the cold water. Was it just her overactive imagination or was he really going to kiss her? Did he regret almost kissing her or the interruption? Her shoulders sagged. Now, he's going to Kaitlyn's which she should be glad of but wasn't. She wished her apartment was ready. She couldn't be trusted anywhere near the man

CHAPTER THIRTEEN

Brianna stood in front of her bathroom mirror applying her makeup for the third time. It was Saturday night, finally, and she really was looking forward to going out— if only her blind date and Kaitlyn Schuster weren't going. Wiping off her lipstick and reaching for a different color, Brianna thought about how the night would be if it were just she and John, a thought that crept into her mind often during the past week . She shook her head. *It'd never work.* Running a hand over her hair, Brianna lifted it off her neck. *Maybe I should wear it up.* She reached for a clip and dropped it on the floor when John spoke from the bedroom doorway.

"Are you about ready?" He looked up from his watch.

Brianna noticed his gray eyes darken to near black as they traveled over her, head to toe, before returning to hers. She blushed and swallowed the lump in her throat.

"Is this okay?" She swept her hands down her dress – the dress he had bought for her had quickly become her favorite.

"Perfect," he said, eyes lingering on her lips. He blinked and straightened, indicating she should precede him out of the room.

She took a deep breath as she passed him, filling her senses with the masculine scent of him.

"Do you have a jacket?" John asked. "It's cool this evening."

Brianna shook her head, quickly dismissing her denim jacket and bulky, oversized sweater as totally unsuitable. John opened the coat closet and pulled out a mossy green mohair shawl.

"My mother's," he said, as he placed it around her shoulders.

Brianna smiled her thanks, relishing the warm imprint of his hands more than the soft warmth of the shawl.

"We're meeting your date at the marina but we need to pick up Kaitlyn." He held the door open for her.

So much for the feeling of warmth. However, she was determined to have a good time in spite of Kaitlyn. Who knows, her date could very well be the love of her life. She glanced up at John as they waited for the elevator. *Then, again, probably not.* She sighed.

"You're not nervous, are you?" John looked down at her.

Brianna bit her bottom lip and shook her head.

"Your date is a very nice young man. Did I mention he's Dr. Anderson's son?"

Brianna shook her head again, not trusting herself to speak without squeaking. Maybe she was a little nervous. *Everybody's nervous going on a blind date, aren't they?* She stepped into the elevator.

"He's in medical school at Loyola," John continued as he pushed the button to the ground floor.

She nodded.

John grinned at her. "You **are** nervous." He wrapped an arm around her shoulders and gave her a reassuring squeeze.

Oh, that helps. She gulped. *Better to let him think I'm nervous about the date than weak-kneed over him.* She glanced up and gave him a feeble smile.

"That's better. You'll be fine." He dropped his arm as the doors opened.

Brianna willed herself to walk steadily to the waiting car. She welcomed the assistance of the doorman as he seated her and closed the door. John slid behind the wheel.

"It's the suit," Brianna said.

"The suit?" John glanced at her, eyebrow raised. "What's wrong with my suit?"

"Nothing's wrong with the suit. It's just that with it on you're Mr. Sharp, the boss. Without it you're just a– John." *That didn't sound right.* The corner of John's mouth twitched. "I mean, under the suit you're a man." *Oh, yeah. That sounded better!* The twitch morphed into a grin. "I'll just shut up now," she said, sliding down in her seat and hugging the door handle. *Lord, if You're planning a rapture, now would be a good time.*

The remainder of the drive to Kaitlyn's was in silence except for the occasional chuckle from John causing Brianna to silently rain Irish curses on his head.

"I'll just be a minute," John said, pulling into a space in front of Kaitlyn's brownstone. Brianna nodded, still too mortified to speak.

When he disappeared into the building, Brianna took the opportunity to avoid an awkward moment by switching to the backseat. She picked up her purse, wrapped the shawl more securely around her and opened the door.

Stepping onto the curb she pushed the door shut and reached for the handle on the back door. **Click.** *Oh, great!* She lifted the handle and pulled anyway. *Damn automatic door locks!* She leaned against a lamp post to wait. It shouldn't be long, she thought.

She smiled at a woman pushing a baby in a stroller and a man walking his dog. She shifted from her left foot to her right. She ignored the whistles from a couple of teenage boys across the street. The woman with the baby came back with a sack of groceries. The man with the dog came back with a bag that wasn't groceries. She wrinkled her nose and shifted her feet again.

Just as she finished counting the windows in the building across the street she heard, "What's she doing here?"

Brianna pulled herself up to her full five-feet-four, with the aid of high heels, mustered a smile and turned to face Kaitlyn and John.

"We're double dating," John said. Turning to Brianna, he asked, "Why are you standing on the curb?"

Brianna glared at him. Kaitlyn glared at Brianna.

"How nice," Kaitlyn said to John. She did not look like she thought it was at all nice.

189

"Ms. Schuster." Brianna said.

"Oh, please call me Kaitlyn. We're not at the office." Her lips formed a saccharin smile.

Lord, control my tongue!

Before Brianna could temper an answer, Kaitlyn turned her attention back to John, leaning toward him and claiming his arm.

Brianna wrinkled her nose. John disengaged himself, unlocked the doors and opened the front door for Kaitlyn. When she was seated he opened the back door for Brianna giving her a look that said, "Behave yourself."

She returned it with an "I will if she will" look of her own. John's eyes narrowed in warning. Brianna jerked the door shut.

Mercifully, the ride to the marina was short. Kaitlyn's flirting was nauseating and would have been a real threat to Brianna's determination to have a good time if she hadn't taken so much pleasure at seeing John's discomfort.

They pulled up in front of the restaurant. The valet simultaneously opened both passenger doors and attempted to assist Kaitlyn who ignored his proffered hand and tossed her head toward the backseat, indicating he should help Brianna. She flashed Brianna a triumphant look as John reached for her hand. Resisting the temptation to stick her tongue out, Brianna accepted the valet's offered hand. Kaitlyn possessively latched onto John's arm thwarting his attempt to turn to Brianna, leaving her to trail behind them.

Once inside, Brianna stood to the side as John spoke to the Maitre d'.

"Your date is waiting in the lounge," John said stepping back to allow the ladies to precede him into the dim and crowded room.

A young man seated at the bar turned as they entered the room, waved a greeting to John and walked toward them. He was tall, though not as tall as John, had sandy blond hair and a friendly smile. Brianna liked him instantly. The men shook hands and John introduced Kaitlyn. He turned to Brianna. "Brianna, this is Brian Anderson."

Brian clasped her hand and held it.

"Brian and Brianna. How cute is that!" Kaitlyn said. "You make such a perfectly adorable couple."

They both blushed slightly, glanced at each other self consciously and laughed.

"Thank you," Brianna said, lacing her arm through Brian's. "I think so, too." She tilted her head up meeting Brian's eyes with a twinkle and squeezed his arm.

"I believe our table is ready." John scowled.

Kaitlyn attempted to grasp John's hand but he took hold of her elbow and followed the Maitre d'.

They were seated at a table overlooking Lake Michigan and handed menus. The Maitre d' gave John the wine list.

"Is white wine good for everyone?" he asked, when the waiter stopped at their table. Brian and Brianna nodded.

"I'd prefer a merlot," Kaitlyn said.

"A bottle of Sauvignon Blanc and the lady will have a glass of merlot."

"I've changed my mind," Kaitlyn said. "I'll have a Gray Goose martini, with two olives not onions."

Brianna and Brian stole quick glances and hid smiles behind napkins. Brianna felt a foot nudge hers under the table and looked at John. He narrowed his eyes, Brianna widened hers. They missed Kaitlyn's puzzled look.

"That certainly is a colorful dress, Brianna. Wherever did you get it?" Kaitlyn asked.

"I– it–" she glanced at John. "It was a gift."

"Well, it's simply darling."

"I think the color matches her eyes," John said.

Kaitlyn looked at John then turned back to Brianna.

"I could show you how to apply make-up to enhance them," Kaitlyn said.

Brianna looked up but before she could voice the retort itching to leap off the tip of her tongue, John responded, "Her eyes are gorgeous the way they are."

Brian looked at her intently, "Yes, they are beautiful."

Kaitlyn and Brianna both reddened but for much different reasons.

Brianna studied the menu until the waiter returned with their drinks.

"Are you ready to order?" he asked.

"Brianna?" John indicated for her to order.

"I'll have the shrimp scampi, please and a salad with ranch dressing."

The waiter looked at Brian.

"That sounds good. I'll have the same."

"Kaitlyn?" John said.

"I want the grilled salmon, lightly grilled but not undercooked and with lemon on the side. No butter. Sautéed vegetables but only if they are fresh and not frozen. I want a Cesar Salad with the dressing on the side. And bring another one of these." Kaitlyn tilted her glass toward the waiter before taking a sip.

Brianna hid behind her napkin covering a giggle while casting a sideways glance at Brian who didn't bother to hide his grin. Brianna felt her foot nudged again and, again, it was accompanied by John's narrowed gaze. Brianna frowned and, this time, returned a warning look. *Next time you get a kick in the shin.*

Kaitlyn drained her glass and set it on the table with a thump.

John placed his order, then looked at Brianna and Brian who appeared to be having an intimate conversation.

"So, Brian, your father tells me medical school is going well for you."

Brian looked up. "Yes, sir. It's going very well. I start my residency next fall at Johns Hopkins."

"That is impressive. Congratulations." Even Kaitlyn looked impressed.

"Thank you, sir. I'm lucky to have been accepted."

"I'm sure luck had little to do with it," Brianna said, laying a hand on his arm and giving him a warm smile. John frowned.

Kaitlyn laid her hand on John's arm. "John, you are the envy of men twice your age. You've built an impressive business."

"Excuse me," John said, reaching for his glass of wine, effectively removing Kaitlyn's hand. "I didn't build it singlehandedly. I have an amazing art department for one thing." He smiled at Brianna.

Kaitlyn reached for her empty glass. "Where is that waiter with my drink?"

John refilled the wine glasses as the waiter returned with Kaitlyn's martini.

"It's about time," she said, grabbing the glass before the waiter could set it down.

Brian and Brianna exchanged glances.

Again, Brianna felt a nudge on her foot.

"Ouch," John jumped and glared at Brianna.

"Oh, I'm sorry. Was that your leg?" Brianna said, sweetly.

Kaitlyn looked at John, then Brianna, and back at John. John picked up his wine as Kaitlyn slid her hand onto his thigh. He jerked and the wine sloshed onto Kaitlyn's dress. She jumped up with a shriek as wine ran quickly into her cleavage. John's wide-eyed stare had Brianna nearly hysterical with laughter.

"Well, at least it's white," Brianna said when she composed herself.

"Brianna, come with me to the ladies' room." Kaitlyn said.

"No, that's okay. I don't need to go."

"I insist," Kaitlyn said through clenched teeth.

Brianna glared at John. "Well, since you put it that way, how can I refuse." John and Brian stood.

John held Brianna back and whispered in her ear, "Watch yourself."

Brianna freed her arm and followed Kaitlyn.

"This dress is pure silk and it's ruined," Kaitlyn said, as she stood in front of the sink.

"It's hardly noticeable. I'm sure a good cleaners can take care of it."

"What's going on between you and John?" Kaitlyn demanded.

Brianna stopped applying lip-gloss and stared at Kaitlyn's reflection. "There's nothing going on. What do you mean?"

"I think you know exactly what I mean." Kaitlyn turned to face Brianna.

"Not a clue," Brianna dropped the lip-gloss into her purse and turned to leave.

Kaitlyn brushed past and stood in her path. "You know, I can make your life miserable."

"I'm sure you can." Brianna tossed her hair and swished through the door.

The men stood as they returned to the table. Brianna avoided looking at John and gave Brian a grimace. In their absence the food had been served.

"That was good timing," Brian said, holding Brianna's chair.

"This looks great," Brianna said.

John took a bite of his steak. "Hmmm, this is delicious. Would you like a bite?" He asked Brianna.

At her nod, he cut another bite, reached across the table and fed it to her. Kaitlyn looked from one to the other.

"I'd like a bite," Kaitlyn simpered.

'I didn't think you ate red meat." John cut another piece and moved his plate toward her.

She glared. "You're right. I don't." She picked up her fork and viciously stabbed her salmon.

"I believe it's already dead, Kaitlyn," Brianna quipped.

Brian burst out laughing. Unfortunately, John had just taken another bite of his filet and started choking. Brian jumped up and preformed the Heimlich maneuver on him. The morsel lodged in John's throat flew out and landed right in the middle of Kaitlyn's salmon.

Brianna reached over and removed the steak from Kaitlyn's plate.

"John, Kaitlyn doesn't eat red meat."

Kaitlyn threw down her fork and pushed her chair back, nearly knocking it over.

"I've had enough," she said. "John, take me home." She picked up her purse. "Now!"

"For Pete's sake, Kaitlyn. Give him a minute to catch his breath," Brian said.

John took a couple of swallows of water and pushed back his chair. "I'm fine. Not everyone is finished eating, Kaitlyn."

"Well, I'm quite finished. If you won't take me, get me a cab."

"But, Brianna..." John started to say.

"For heaven's sake, John. She's a big girl. Let Brian take her home."

"I'd be happy to drive her home, sir," Brian said.

John frowned at Brian and turned to Brianna.

"That's fine. Brian can take me home." She smiled at Brian.

"Fine," John said. "Do you have your key?"

Brianna shook her head.

"I'll leave mine with the security guard."

Kaitlyn stopped, raised her brows and dropped her jaw. "What?" she shrieked.

"I'll explain later, Kaitlyn," John said, guiding Kaitlyn quickly through the tables to the exit before she caused a scene.

When they disappeared from sight Brian turned to Brianna. "You live with him?"

"Well– sort of – yes. It's a long story."

Between bites Brianna told Brian her tale and before they were finished eating both were laughing.

"I'll bet this is one blind date you won't soon forget," Brianna said.

"And, it's a bet you'd easily win," Brian said, taking her hand.

* * * *

Brianna eased the door closed and locked it, careful not to disturb John.

"Do you know what time it is?" A voice boomed from a corner of the dark living room.

She jumped and turned. Leaning against the closed door, she willed her galloping heart to slow. When she could breathe again, she retorted, "No, but if you'll turn on a light, I'll look at the clock for you."

"Very funny. It's three AM." John rose, switched on a lamp and moved to lean against the back of the sofa, bracing an arm on either side. "Where have you been?"

"I was with Brian." She straightened. "I wasn't aware I had a curfew."

"I know you were with Brian, and you don't have a curfew, but you should be considerate of someone waiting up for you."

"I didn't know you were going to wait up." Brianna took a step toward him. "Why did you?"

"I didn't think you would be this late. I was concerned. The club closed at one. Where were you?"

"Do you want details or will the highlights do because I'm really sleepy." She moved toward her bedroom door.

John looked at her intently for a moment. "Highlights will do."

Brianna attempted to smooth her windswept hair. "We stayed at the club dancing until it closed. After that, we took a walk along the shore."

John took a step toward her. "So, you like Brian."

"Yes. He's very nice." She noticed John's frown and narrowed eyes. "What? You don't like him?"

"Of course, I like him, otherwise I wouldn't have chosen him for your date. But I wouldn't expect you to like him so much on a first date."

Brianna studied her toes for a few seconds before looking at him. "Oh, I get it. You didn't have a good time and you're upset because I did."

"That's ridiculous." John turned and walked toward the patio door.

"Oh, so you did have a good time?"

"No. That's beside the point. We're talking about you." He slid the door open. "Come to think of it, this whole thing is your fault."

Brianna paused with a hand on her doorknob and turned back to face him. "My fault?" She crossed the room. "How is it my fault?"

201

"You insisted I ask Kaitlyn out." He looked down at her.

"Then it's your fault for listening to me. You know her better than I do." Brianna stalked back to her room. John followed and caught her by the elbow turning her around before she could open the door.

"Tell me more about your date." His eyes scanned her tousled hair.

"Can this wait until morning? I'm really tired."

"Did he kiss you?" he said, focusing on her lips.

Brianna jerked her head up. "I don't see how that's any of your business."

"It's not but I want to know."

She ran her tongue across her lower lip. "Why?" she said, conscious of their bodies nearly touching but unaware of which one had moved.

"I don't know," John said, lowering his head.

Brianna backed up until the doorknob jabbed her spine.

"Well, if you must know, we made mad, passionate love in the sand."

John stepped back and glared at her. Brianna glared back.

He grabbed his suit coat from the back of the sofa and swung it over his shoulder. The strong scent of Obsession struck Brianna as he turned toward his room.

Brianna sneezed and waved a hand in front of her face. "Smells like you had a good time." She walked to the patio door. "I need some fresh air."

John stopped. "What's that supposed to mean?" He followed her onto the balcony.

"You have Kaitlyn's trademark all over you. Did you kiss her?" She moved to the balustrade and leaned back against it striking John's favorite pose, arms folded across her chest, feet crossed at the ankles, and waited for his answer.

"And, if I did, would you care?" John advanced.

Brianna moved her hand up to her throat.

"I– no." She shook her head, averting her eyes. "I couldn't care less what you do or who you do it with." Turning toward the lake, she grasped the railing for support lest she be struck dead by a truth gnome.

"I think you're lying," John said, so close his breath stirred her hair.

Brianna whirled around and pushed at his chest.

"How dare you–" Her words were cut short when John pulled her to him.

His mouth crushed hers. John's hand tunneled beneath her hair to grasp her head while his other arm molded her softness to his hard frame. Breathing became impossible. Her arms encircled his neck. Coherent thought abandoned her. Her feet dangled freely above the terrace floor. Sandals fell unheeded. Time ceased to exist. Heat consumed them.

As suddenly as it began, it ended. John set her down and peeled her arms from his neck. He turned his back, thrusting his hands through his hair before bracing them on the rail. Brianna sank onto a chaise, not sure what was real and what was imagined. She drew much needed air and tested her legs for strength before standing.

She opened her mouth. Something between a squeak and a sob escaped.

Without turning, John said, "Go to bed, Brianna."

"John, I–"

"Go, Brianna. Now." She fled to her room.

CHAPTER FOURTEEN

Brianna stared at the ceiling. She'd barely slept. Every time her eyes closed her lips recalled the searing heat of his kiss. She tossed between savoring the feeling and rationalizing it. Finally coming to the conclusion that it was born of frustration and anger. Though why John was angry remained a mystery.

Footsteps paused outside her room as light began to peek through the drapes. She closed her eyes and held her breath. A few seconds later the steps resumed. The front door opened and closed.

Breathing a sigh of relief, she reached for her phone and called Carly.

Half an hour later Brianna sat in a small beach front bistro stirring a cup of tea and staring at the lake. Carly sat opposite her and slid a muffin across the table. Brianna pushed it back, shaking her head.

"I've been here five minutes and you haven't said a word," Carly said, pushing the muffin back to Brianna. "I assume you didn't ask me to meet you so I could watch you stare out the window."

"He kissed me." Brianna continued stirring her now cold tea.

"Who kissed you? Your blind date? And, that's bad because…?"

"John."

Carly set her cup down, sloshing coffee onto the table. A smile played at the corner of her mouth. "And, that's bad because…?"

Brianna looked up at her. "Because he was angry." She averted her gaze. "And I don't know why."

"Brianna, look at me." She reached over and turned Brianna's face toward her. "Nobody kisses someone because they're angry. Tell me everything. I need details, girl!"

Reliving the scene evoked feelings similar to those she experienced during the kiss but she suppressed them, choosing to focus on the negative. "He pushed me away. I think he regretted it. Anyway, it didn't mean anything. He was just angry. I don't know how I'm going to face him." Brianna hid her face behind her hands, then pushed her hair back. She gave Carly a cheerless smile and released a shaky breath.

Carly studied her for a moment before speaking. "I don't think he regrets kissing you. And, I don't think it was anger. I think he's jealous."

"Jealous! You're insane, Carly. Why would you think that?"

"He waited up for you, didn't he? He asked you if you liked Brian, then got angry when you said you did. He asked you if Brian kissed you. Think about it, Bree. Why would he want to know that?"

"I don't know." Brianna slumped down in her chair.

"Oh, I think you do. You just won't admit it." Carly leaned back. "You're in love with him — we both know that. Why is it so hard to imagine that he might feel the same?"

"Because." — Brianna searched Carly's face for answers but only got a smug look. "It just is."

Carly moved to the seat next to Brianna and took both her hands in hers. "Listen to me. You can't think of a single reason, can you?" Brianna shook her head and Carly continued. " It's quite possible, probable even, that he feels the same way. Talk to him."

"And what, exactly, am I supposed to say to him?" She pulled her hands from Carly's. "Oh, John, by the way, are you in love with me? Yeah, that'll work."

"Now who's being silly?" Carly quipped.

"Why don't you come home with me and you can ask him?" Brianna said, half hoping she would.

"I would but," she looked at her watch and stood. "Gee, would you look at the time. I have to pick Rob up in twenty minutes. Call me later."

"I'll call you a chicken."

Carly clucked all the way to the door. She turned and blew a kiss to Brianna before walking out. Brianna blew a raspberry at her.

After spending the afternoon kicking pebbles along the lake shore, Brianna was no more clear-headed than when she started. She carefully picked her way along the rocky shoreline back to the condo. The sidewalk would have been faster but she wasn't particularly in a hurry – actually she wanted to prolong the inevitable as long as possible.

"Talk to him," Carly had said. Words swam around in her head but they refused to come together in coherent sentences. She picked up a flat rock and skipped it across the surface, wishing she could be a dragonfly riding on it.

All too soon she arrived at the high rise. She took a deep breath, straightened her shoulders and entered the building. After taking some time to chat with the doorman and the security guard, she punched the button for the elevator. It opened immediately. *Just my luck.* She got in and pushed the button for John's floor. The elevator shot to the twenty-fifth floor like a souped-up Mustang.

Digging her key out of her pocket, she walked to the door and leaned her head on it while fitting the key into the lock. Before she could turn the key, the door opened and she tumbled head-first into John's stomach sending them crashing to the floor.

So much for sneaking into my room.

Brianna rolled off him and sat up.

"Oh, my gosh. I'm so sorry. Are you okay?" She looked at John who struggled to catch his breath.

"It's okay. I'm getting used to it." John stood and offered a hand to help Brianna to her feet. "Where have you been? I was beginning to worry about you."

"I went for a walk." Brianna answered. She noticed John's raised eyebrow and added, "A long one."

"Dinner is nearly ready. Are you hungry?"

She shook her head. "I ate a hot dog on the beach. I'm going to take a shower." She turned toward her room.

"Come out to the terrace when you're through. We need to talk."

Scratch Plan B.

She really just wanted to go to bed but she knew she couldn't avoid him for a whole week until her apartment was ready.

Brianna nodded.

Forty minutes later she stepped onto the terrace barefoot, her hair still damp. John watched her approach. He offered her a glass of wine from the bottle on the table. She declined – better not confuse her brain more than it already was.

John leaned back against the balustrade and sipped his wine. Brianna squirmed under his scrutiny.

"I know what you want to talk about and it's okay. I understand. You were frustrated and angry. It didn't mean anything." Brianna avoided his eyes, leaning on the railing beside him.

John was silent for a few minutes before he walked to the table and set his glass down. He turned toward her.

"It meant something to me."

Brianna looked up and met his eyes.

He continued. "For the record, I was not angry." He took a step toward her. She ran her tongue over her dry lower lip. He took another step, then another until there was no space left between them. He reached up and traced his thumb along the path her tongue had taken. His fingers splayed beneath her ear, then traveled to the back of her neck. Brianna's heart banged against her ribs, a small moan escaped.

"Please tell me it meant something to you, too," he said.

Brianna stood paralyzed. He lowered his head until she inhaled his breath and his mouth closed over hers. Her hand traveled up his chest, she felt the steady beat of his heart before raising on her tiptoes to circle his neck. Her other hand found its way to his back where she stroked the hard smooth muscles.

The pressure of his mouth increased. He cradled her head with one hand and caressed her spine with the other. His tongue traced her parted lips before pushing inside to tango with hers.

She whimpered when John left her mouth to rain kisses along her jaw, over her eyes and the little hollow beneath her ear. She nipped his earlobe. He traced her ear with his tongue. She wrapped a leg around his bringing them ever closer. John inhaled sharply and reclaimed her lips in a searing kiss. She could no longer think. She could only feel.

John kissed the hollow between her neck and shoulder before stepping back. He ran his hands up and down her arms. Smiling into her up-turned face, he took her hand and led her to the chaise, pulling her down beside him.

"This isn't exactly what I had in mind when I said we needed to talk." His voice was gravelly. He laughed at her puzzled expression. "Oh, it was in my mind, but I wanted to talk first."

He wrapped an arm around her and cradled her head in the crook of his neck and kissed her temple. The moon bathed them in a glow as if it were hung just for them. Brianna shivered.

"Are you cold?" He rubbed her arm.

She shook her head. "You want to talk *now*?" She squeaked. She cleared her throat and reached for the half full wine glass on the table.

John chuckled. "I have a couple of things I'd like to say, yes."

Brianna raised the glass to her lips. "Like?"

"For starters, I love you."

She set the glass down with a shaky hand and turned to stare at him.

"You what?" She was certain she hadn't heard him right.

"I love you. And, I don't want to live without you."

Brianna threw herself on top of him and, framing his face with both hands, kissed him.

John rolled her beneath him and raised up on one arm.

"I take it you feel—?"

Brianna brought his lips to hers.

* * * *

Brianna woke when John brushed the hair off her neck and kissed her nape. His arm encircled her, drawing her close to his warm body. Rolling onto her back, she smiled as his mouth slowly made its way along her collarbone and over her jaw before finally claiming her lips. Brianna purred.

A muffled tone sounded from the floor. John raised his head, his eyes dark with passion. He grumbled and rolled over.

"I have to answer this." He retrieved the offending cell phone from the pocket of his crumpled pants and sat on the edge of the bed.

Cool air rushed to fill the void where John's body had been. Brianna frowned and wrapped the sheet around her as she stood.

"Calm down. I'll be there as soon as I can." John said into the phone.

She walked around the end of the bed heading for the door. John grasped the sheet and pulled her down beside him. Not wanting to listen to the conversation, she tried to stand but he put his arm around her waist. She knitted her eyebrows and nodded toward the bathroom. He released her, trailing his hand across her back. She gathered the large sheet and left the room, closing the door softly behind her.

Donning John's robe, she waited a few minutes before returning to the bedroom. John sat on the bed, elbows resting on his knees, his head in his hands. He raked a hand through his hair and patted a spot beside him for her to sit.

"That was my mother on the phone. My father's had a heart attack. I'm all they have. I need to be there."

"Oh, no. I'm so sorry. You must be terribly worried," she said, placing a hand on his arm.

"I'm concerned but I leave the worrying to my mother. She's very good at it."

He raised his head, brought his hand to her cheek, tracing his thumb over her lower lip.

"Is there anything I can do?" Brianna asked.

"Yes, please. While I shower and pack, would you make a reservation for me on the first American flight to Tucson? First class." He gave her the password to his Advantage account.

She glanced at the clock on the nightstand. Was it really only seven a.m.?

Brianna went to the den to book the flight. Grabbing the confirmation from the printer, she went back to his room.

She trailed her hand over the bed as she wandered to the window. The sun continued its journey blazing a trail of gold across the lake. A few boats were leaving the nearby marina and cars rushed along the street below. John came up to stand beside her, draping his arm around her shoulder.

"Great timing," he said.

Brianna nodded, stroking his hand.

"You're on a non-stop flight that leaves O'Hare at 9:45. That will get you into Tucson at 11:30." She handed him the itinerary. "I called for a cab."

"Thanks, Bree. That's perfect." He folded the paper and tucked it into his breast pocket. "My bag is packed. I just have to get my shaving gear."

When he returned, he once again put his arm around her and walked to the front door. He dropped his arm from her shoulders and hooked his finger in the V of her robe, drawing her to him. She raised up on her toes to meet his lips. Breaking contact, he sighed heavily and rested his forehead on hers. He glanced at his watch.

"I have to get going but I'll call you tonight.

"Have a good flight. I'll be praying for your dad."

He stroked his knuckles down her cheek.

"I love you," he said and closed the door between them.

Brianna leaned against the door, hardly daring to believe how much her life had changed in less than twelve hours. She glanced at the clock on the mantel. There was no way she could get to work on time. Toying with the idea of calling in sick and spending the day snuggled in John-scented sheets, she pushed away from the door. *If only the housekeeper wasn't coming today. It wouldn't do for her to catch me in John's bed.*

She called her supervisor and told her she would be late due to transportation problems—

which was true as she needed to figure out the L schedule online.

Arriving at the office only an hour late, she checked in with Miss Davis and got her assignment. She stuck her head in Carly's cubicle before going to her own.

"Morning."

Carly glanced up. "Hey, you're la—Oh. My. God." She jumped up from her desk and wrapped Brianna in a fierce bear hug.

Brianna extricated herself. "What? I'm just late. It's not like I went missing or anything."

"You're absolutely glowing." Carly held her at arm's length. "That could mean only one thing."

Brianna felt the color rushing to her face despite her efforts to remain cool. "I don't know what you're talking about." She looked at the paper in her hand.

"Oh, yes, you do. Look at me." Carly grasped her jaw, turning her face to face. "I'm your best friend, remember? Talk to me."

"All right, all right. At lunch. Miss Davis is looking this way. I have to get to work."

She backed into her cubicle leaving a grinning Carly behind. She'd have to work on her poker face before she became the latest hot topic for the gossip team.

Brianna groaned when she saw the name of the account executive, Kaitlyn Schuster. *Why did I get this assignment?*

At noon, Carly poked her head around the partition between them. "What're you doodling there?"

"Nothing," Brianna answered. "Would you believe I've been given the new Saks' campaign to work on? It should have gone to Liv."

"She's pretty tied up with the Bloomingdale account. Who's the suit?"

"Kaitlyn."

"Ahh, well, there ya' go." Carly grinned.

Miss Davis met them as they were leaving for lunch. "Ms. Schuster wants to see you in her office at one."

"Yes, ma'am," Brianna said. When the supervisor was out of earshot, she mumbled. "Great! Just freakin' great."

* * * *

After lunch Brianna shuffled The Green Mile to Kaitlyn's office.

She knocked lightly on the frame of the open door.

Kaitlyn rose from her chair and looked down her perfect nose, ice-pick heels giving her nearly a foot advantage over Brianna,. They assessed each other for several seconds across the desk before Kaitlyn spoke. "John left me in charge while he is away."

Brianna met her frosty eyes and opened her mouth to challenge Kaitlyn's statement. For once, she thought better of it.

"That's what you called me in here for?" Brianna cocked one brow.

Kaitlyn narrowed her gaze. "I expect preliminary drawings for the Saks' campaign on my desk by Thursday morning. Can you handle that?"

"I'm sure it won't be a problem, Ms. Schuster."

"It's a great opportunity for you, *Bree*," Kaitlyn's patronizing tone stiffened Brianna's spine.

"Yes, it is. Thank you so much for the favor, *Ms. Schuster.*" She nearly gagged on the words and forced the corners of her mouth up.

Kaitlyn stepped back, her eyes frigid. "If you disappoint me, *Ms. Ryan,* I'll have no choice but to inform Mr. Sharp." Bracing her arms, she leaned over her desk until she was nose to nose with Brianna. "Is that clear?"

"Crystal clear, Ms Schuster." Brianna shot the icicle daggers back, turned and stomped out of the room.

Carly looked up when Brianna returned. "I see that went well."

Brianna rolled her eyes, opened her mouth a couple of times then waggled her head and retreated to her cubby hole.

CHAPTER FIFTEEN

John called as she was finishing dinner. Her heart turned over at the sound of his voice.

"You sound tired." She detected the weariness in his tone.

"It's been a very long day."

"That it has. How's your father?"

"He's doing pretty well. The doctors want to run more tests in the morning. If they come out all right he'll be able to go home on Wednesday. I'm planning to stay until Saturday, if I can stand it that long. My mother is already driving me insane."

"She's just worried about your father."

"You don't know my mother; she's the kind who makes coffee nervous."

221

Brianna laughed. "Be patient. She'll be happy when your father gets home."

"I'm sure she will. She'll have two of us to fuss about. How are you doing?" John asked.

"I had a little trouble figuring out the L but I was only an hour late."

"You could drive my car. The valet has the keys."

"I never had the chance to learn to drive." She traced a fingernail along the pattern in the granite counter top.

"Really? We'll have to work on that when I get home."

"Great. That will be fun—at least, for me." She chuckled.

"I'm sure it will be for me, too." John assured her. "I miss you. I'll call you tomorrow. I love you."

"Love you, too. 'Night." Brianna hugged the phone a moment before laying it on the nightstand.

It was too early to go to bed but it was just the right time for a long bubble bath. She lit scented candles while the tub filled.

Securing her hair on top of her head, she stepped into the tub and relaxed into the foamy water. The little shell-shaped pillow cradled her head and her eyes closed.

Images of John forced visions of Kaitlyn to the dark corner of her brain where thoughts she refused to acknowledge resided. John loved her and that was all that mattered.

When the water finally turned too cold to be comfortable, she sighed, stood and wrapped a bath sheet around her shivering body. Pulling the clips from her hair, she dropped the towel and climbed naked into John's bed luxuriating in the subtle but intoxicating, male scent surrounding her.

. * *

By Thursday, Brianna's week had settled into a routine. John's nightly calls were the highlight of each day, sending her to sleep with warm, fuzzy feelings. Working on the Saks account and avoiding Kaitlyn provided challenges that passed the time quickly. *Only two more days.* She dug her pass out of her purse and boarded the "L."

A note stuck to her monitor stated, "I want to see you in my office immediately. K. S."

Brianna threw her purse into the bottom drawer and slammed it shut.

Carly appeared above the partition. "I take it you saw the note." She grinned.

223

Brianna glared. "She wants to see me 'immediately'– as in get your sorry bum in here now." She flopped into the chair spinning it to face the computer and ripped the large pink sticky off the screen. "I'm really beginning to hate Post-its." She crumpled it into a ball and tossed it back at Carly over her head.

It took three tries to log onto her computer. She knew this was coming but to be rudely summoned caught her off guard. It whipped up her Irish blood. She pulled the drawings from the top drawer, scanned them into her computer, grabbed her purse and left the cubicle.

"If I'm not back in an hour, send in the troops," she said to Carly before trudging to the Green Mile.

Kaitlyn cradled her phone against her shoulder and motioned for Brianna to enter.

"I'll call you back." Kaitlyn replaced the receiver and stood. "It took you long enough to get here. Don't tell me you were late – again."

Brianna opened her mouth. The words that formed in her brain were unfit to utter in English but sounded pleasant enough in Gaelic especially when spoken with a sweet smile. Kaitlyn furrowed her brows.

"I was on time, ma'am."

"Humph." Kaitlyn snatched the folder from Brianna's hand so fast her fingers burned. "Are these the Saks drawings?"

Brianna nodded. She stood with her hands clasped tightly around her purse strap to keep them from wrapping around Kaitlyn's skinny neck.

One by one, Kaitlyn dropped the sketches onto her desk. As the last one hit the pile, she looked up.

Her narrowed gaze pierced Brianna. "These are junk," she sneered. "If this is the kind of work you do, I don't know how you keep your job." She paused. "Oh. Right. Sleeping with the boss does have advantages."

Brianna took a step back, her jaw dropped. Even the bad words abandoned her. The heat that infused her from toes to forehead betrayed her.

Kaitlyn gasped. "So, I've hit a nerve." She sat and leaned back in her chair. "Well, well, well." She steepled her fingers beneath her chin. A smug look crossed her face.

When the words swirling in her mind fought to escape, Brianna felt like she'd throw them up. She turned to leave.

"You're not going to deny it?" Kaitlyn snarled.

Brianna halted and slowly turned to face her.

"You wouldn't believe me if I did." Brianna pushed her hair from her face and raised her chin. "But quite frankly, Ms. Schuster, whether I am or not is none of your business." Green eyes matched the frigid tone of the blue ones. The blue ones lowered and Brianna pivoted toward the door. At the sound of ripping paper, she squared her shoulders.

"Ms. Ryan!" Kaitlyn's menacing shout stopped Brianna but she refused to turn choosing instead to raise her eyes to the ceiling. "You're fired."

The words nearly ruptured her eardrums. The knot in her stomach twisted. Whirling to face the enemy, Brianna prepared for battle. She marched across the room, stopping in the face of evil. At this point, surrender– or at least retreat– seemed a better option.

Brianna took a deep breath. "I doubt you have the authority to fire me, Kaitlyn but I am going to leave." She grabbed her empty folder from the desktop. "You have a nice day."

"Why you insolent little–"

Brianna didn't wait to hear the end of that sentence.

CHAPTER SIXTEEN

John's flight landed at O'Hare one day and fifteen minutes early. He glanced at his watch. *Seven-fifteen* - with any luck he'd be home by eight. Hitching his bag up on his shoulder he walked quickly down the concourse, thankful he didn't have to wait at the baggage carousel. Several pairs of admiring eyes followed as long strides carried him to the entrance but his thoughts were focused on a pair of green eyes. Side-stepping a baby carriage he increased his pace to a waiting taxi.

* * * *

Brianna woke with a start when someone knocked on the front door. *Who could that be?* It was almost dark. She got up from the chaise on the terrace, picked up the book that had slid off her lap and walked through the living room to the entry. The large clock above the fireplace read eight-fifteen. She peeked through the peephole. *Oh, my God!* In an effort to gather her jumbled thoughts and control her temper, she leaned against the door for a moment.

Brianna jerked the door open.

"What the bloody hell are you doing here?" So much for temper control.

"Nice to see you, too, Breeze."

"How did you know where I was?"

"Whoa, Breeze, is that anyway to greet an old friend?

"You're not a friend. You're a rotten liar and a thief!"

Eric brushed past her and entered the condo looking around appreciatively. He whistled.

"Livin' with the boss has its advantages, I see."

"I'm not 'livin' with the boss.' He's letting me stay here until I have enough money for a place of my own. You moved out and stole all my money. Remember?"

"I didn't steal *your* money. It was a joint account." His grin was pure evil. "I followed you home yesterday. Left work a little early, didn't you? I guess when the boss is away the mistress can play."

Brianna's hand itched to slap the smirk off his face. "How did...? Mr. Sharp will be home any minute."

"Now who's lying? I overheard you tell Carly he wouldn't be home until tomorrow night?"

Crap. Brianna glanced around for a weapon. Too bad John never left anything—like a nine-iron or machete—lying around. She kicked herself for leaving her cell phone on the terrace. A well-placed knee could bring him down—or just make him angry.

"Leave, Eric." *Before I kill you.*

"Something tells me you're not all that happy to see me."

"Go." Brianna glared at him, and gestured to the door.

"I'm really sorry, Breezy. I don't know what I was thinking. I guess I just got scared of the commitment." He flashed his most charming grin at her. "If you could forgive me maybe we could try again."

"You're crazy." The rein on her temper slipped a little more. "It's been a month and you haven't even tried to contact me. If I never see you again, it will be too soon. You left me homeless and penniless. Why on earth would I want you back?"

"Yeah, I guess it'd be hard to give all this up but I've got some things in the works. I'll be living like this soon. We had some good times, Breeze. Besides this," he swept his arm around the room, "what's he got that I haven't?"

"You haven't got time for me to make a list. You're leaving." Brianna held the door open.

"I don't think so. I like it here."

"We have nothing more to discuss." Bile bubbled in her throat as panic crept in.

"I think there is and we have plenty of time." Eric reached behind her and shoved the door closed. Smelling the whiskey on his breath, panic stopped creeping and raced through her body. She reached for the intercom button to call security but Eric grabbed her wrist and pulled her toward the sofa.

He sat, dragging her down beside him. Stretching his free arm along the back, he propped his booted feet on the glass coffee table. Brianna fought to free her wrist from his vice-like grip. Eric grabbed her other wrist and twisted her arms behind her, forcing her across his lap. Grasping both her arms in one hand, he grabbed a handful of hair with his other hand holding her still as his mouth descended toward hers. Brianna struggled but each movement caused sharp pains to move up her arms to her twisted shoulders.

Eric jerked on her hair until she cried out in pain. He rolled her onto her back, pinning her arms beneath her and sprawled on top of her.

"That's it, you little spit-fire. Tell me you want me. You know you do." He claimed her mouth before she could scream. Brianna continued to resist, turning her head painfully from side to side in a futile effort to avoid his consuming mouth. She had never seen Eric like this. He had been controlling and demanding but never violent. *It must be the whiskey.* Biting down hard on his lower lip, she tasted blood. Eric yelled and raised his head but did not release his grip on her arms or hair. He tugged hard on her hair causing a burning sensation in her scalp. She cried out.

Brianna heard the front door click shut. Eric slowly raised his head to peer over the back of the sofa. He released her and she sat up, disheveled, and looked into a pair of smoldering gray eyes.

"Hey, we weren't expecting you back until tomorrow," Eric said.

"Obviously," John said, his eyes leaving Brianna's and landing on Eric. "Out."

As he walked back to the door he caught a glimpse of the unmade bed in her room and turned his eyes, now icy, back to Brianna.

"Get out, now!" he said to Eric as he opened the door.

"See ya', Babe." Eric planted a kiss on her lips. She noticed his lip was swollen where she had bit it. *Good.* Thankfully he had enough sense to leave without a fight, one he certainly would have lost. Running a shaky hand through her tousled hair, she looked at John. He shoved the door shut barely giving Eric time to get through. He looked at her with a odd mixture of contempt and pain before turning toward his room without saying a word.

"John, I—" Brianna began but John slammed his door before she could finish.

* * * *

Brianna stared at the offending portal a second before charging down the hall. Hearing a thud, she hesitated. *Maybe I should let him calm down a bit.* She withdrew her hand before it touched the knob. Angry muttering filtered through the door. *He has no right*—her hand shot out again but retreated as footsteps approached the door. She turned and stalked to her room.

John threw his bag in the corner and walked to the window. "I trusted her. How could I have been so blind?" he said to his reflection.

He rubbed the back of his neck as he stared toward the lake. *I should talk to her.* He walked to the door and reached for the knob. *No, whatever she has to say can wait until morning.* Jamming his hand in his pocket so it couldn't reach for the door knob again, he paced back to the window. *How could she do this? And in my home!* He smacked the window frame. He turned and stared at the bed. *Only 5 days ago*—he swiped a hand down his face. His heart leapt at the memory. Shaking his head, he strode to the closet and pitched his clothes onto the bench, took a cold shower and got into bed. He was assaulted by the scent of strawberries as soon as his head hit the pillow. *Damn!* He flung the pillow across the room. It didn't matter—her essence surrounded him.

Tears flowed freely as Brianna shut her door. She leaned against it, struggling to breathe. Sliding to the floor, she wrapped her arms around her knees and buried her face. Licking a tear from the corner of her mouth, she got up and grabbed a pillow from the bed hugging it to her chest in an effort to stop the pain. Slow motion footsteps carried her to the window. Her eyes moved from the traffic still bustling below to the moon glistening overhead. Life hadn't stopped. She closed the drapes. Anger and pain battled in her stomach. Turning, she threw the pillow at the bed.

She was hurt by John's reaction and angry at herself for caring so much. She paced back to the window. She understood why he'd gotten the wrong idea from the way Eric acted. Her bed was unmade. That definitely did not look good but it could have been worse. *I could have slept in John's bed like I had a few nights while he was gone and he'd have thought we'd been in there.* Brianna bit her bottom lip.

How could he even think—Eric nearly raped me, probably would have if he hadn't shown up when he did. She'd be thankful for that tomorrow.

She marched back to the door. She'd been convicted by circumstantial evidence, no trial, no defense, just condemned. She was beyond anger - she was livid. She reached for the door knob again.

Shoulders sagging, she stopped, turned and sank onto the edge of her bed. *If he doesn't trust me, how can he love me?* She walked to the closet, opened the door and pulled out her suitcase.

* * * *

John left a trail of broken pencils in his wake as he paced restlessly around his office. He glanced briefly at his secretary as she entered and placed a large cup of coffee on his desk.

"Thanks."

"You look like you could use it."

"It's been a rough week."

"Will you be needing more pencils?"

John looked at the two halves of his latest victim and tossed them on the desktop.

"No, thanks, Sandy." He smiled ruefully.

"Is there anything I can do?"

"No." He paused. "Yes, you can get Ms. Ryan in here."

"Yes, Mr. Sharp."

When she left, John sat down to drink his coffee and wait for Brianna. *Rough week. That's an understatement.* He got up and walked to the window. *It ranks right up there with…with…* He could think of nothing to compare it with. It was the worst weekend of his entire life. Plagued with bad dreams, he had given up trying to sleep. He spent most of the time wearing out his carpet or running along the lakeshore trying to sort out his conflicting emotions – anger, betrayal, frustration and worry. He felt so empty, so alone, so—

A knock on the door accelerated his heart rate. He still didn't know what he was going to say to her. He didn't know whether to fire her or hug her.

"Come in," His voice cracked. He crossed to stand behind his chair.

Sandy opened the door and stepped into his office.

"Ms. Ryan is not here, Mr. Sharp. Miss Davis said she left Thursday morning with no explanation and hasn't been back."

John stared at her in disbelief. That certainly seemed out of character but what did he know?

"Get me Carly Ames. If anyone knows where she is, she will."

"Right away, sir." Sandy backed out of the room and closed the door.

John smacked the back of his chair, sending it spinning, resumed his pacing and broke several more pencils while he waited for Carly. He walked around his desk as she entered.

"Thank you for coming. Please, sit down." He indicated one of the chairs.

"I prefer to stand." Carly met his eyes.

John raised an eyebrow and leaned against the corner of his desk, folding his arms across his chest.

"Do you know where Brianna is?" he asked.

"Yes."

"But you're not going to tell me."

"No."

"Okay. Do you know why she isn't at work?"

"Yes."

They locked eyes for a moment. John straightened, stepping forward.

"I admire your loyalty but I'm worried about her. I want to know if she's okay."

"She's fi—" Carly looked up at John. "No, she's not 'okay.' What makes you think she'd be okay?" Carly's eyes blazed and she took a step forward. "You assumed the worst without even giving her a chance to explain. You hurt her. Bree is the sweetest, most caring, honest and loyal person I know and I don't—"

"She had her boyfriend there," John said, backing up a step.

Carly took another step closer to John. "She did not have her *ex*-boyfriend there. He showed up, unannounced and uninvited, an hour before you arrived."

"I saw—"

"Well, you saw wrong." Carly advanced. "What you should have seen were her swollen and bloody lips and her bruised wrists. He practically raped her and all you could think about was your bruised ego. She loves you and you don't deserve it."

She loves me? John retreated until he backed into his desk. "That doesn't explain why she left work early on Thursday."

Carly took another step forward. "Ms. Schuster fired her, that's why."

Her glare condemned him. She turned and left his office, slamming the door.

John took a minute to absorb this information, crossed to the door, jerked it open and yelled at a startled Sandy, "Get Kaitlyn Schuster in here. Now!"

"Yes, s–" He slammed the door.

John had just finished picking up the numerous broken pencils when Kaitlyn entered and crossed the room.

"Why didn't you call me when you got back?" she pouted. "I've missed you." She reached up and ran a long red fingernail down his cheek.

John grasped her hand and removed it from his face. He turned and walked behind his desk. "This isn't a social call, Kaitlyn."

"If you want to discuss business it's time for the staff meeting. I was just heading there when Mrs. Wilson said you wanted to see me."

Damn! I forgot about the staff meeting. He thought briefly about having Charlie handle it but he'd been gone a week and knew he had to be there. "We'll discuss this after the meeting."

"You could take me to lunch." Kaitlyn suggested.

"This is not a discussion I want to have in public."

* * * *

After the meeting, John spoke to Charlie Meyers briefly before heading for Kaitlyn's office, where he assumed she had gone when she left the meeting early. He walked in without knocking and closed the door firmly behind him.

"Why did you fire Brianna?"

"She was rude to me, and she gave me junk when I asked for drawings for the Saks account."

"Junk?"

"Yes, junk. A cat could have done better sketches."

"Do you happen to have those drawings? I'd like to see them."

"*She* took them."

John motioned for her to get up. "I need to use your computer a minute." He sat down at Kaitlyn's desk. After a brief search of the files, he asked,. "Are these the drawings she gave you?"

Kaitlyn leaned over John's shoulder. "They could be."

"They look like perfectly good preliminary drawings to me."

239

"Hmpf. You would think so."

"I have a feeling you wouldn't have liked anything she gave you." John accused. "You did not have the authority to fire her. If you had a problem, you should have talked to Charlie. He's in charge when I'm away. He was just as surprised as I was about this."

Kaitlyn retrieved a package from the credenza behind her desk. She ripped off the paper wrapping and held up a painting.

"This look familiar?" she asked. "It looks like your little friend is a phony. She copied this painting for the wildlife layout. Do you still think I was wrong to fire her?"

"Where did you get that?" John reached for the painting and carried it to the window to examine it.

"I found it in a little loft gallery off Halsted. The owner said the artist was Eric something. They sold several of his paintings."

"Mind if I borrow this?" John asked.

"Would it matter if I did?"

"No."

"Take it. Doesn't this prove I was right about her? She's a no-talent fake, a conniving, gold-digging little—"

"Stop. Don't say any more."

John turned to leave but Kaitlyn stepped in front of him.

"What about us, John?" She ran her hand up his lapel. "I thought –"

"One date does not make an 'us,' Kaitlyn." He brushed her hand from his jacket.

"But—"

He strode out the door.

* * * *

John hung up the phone, shrugged into his suit jacket and tucked the painting under his arm.

"I'm going out for a couple of hours, Sandy," he said as he walked quickly past his secretary's desk. He waited anxiously for the elevator, stepped into the car before the doors had fully opened and punched the button for the ground floor. By the time the elevator had stopped at the twentieth, nineteenth, fourteenth and twelfth floors he seriously considered investing in an express lift for his floor. He smiled indulgently at each new rider. He finally arrived at the ground floor, walked swiftly to his car and pulled onto the street, heading for the art district a short distance away.

241

He parked at the curb in front of the building Kaitlyn had mentioned and walked up the steep flight of stairs to the loft gallery.

The door jingled when he opened it and a tall, thin young man with a blonde ponytail and goatee greeted him.

"Mr. Sharp?" The young man extended his hand. "I'm Andy, the manager."

"Has he been in yet?" John asked, shaking the young man's hand.

"No, sir, but I expect him soon."

John showed him the painting that Kaitlyn had purchased. "If you look closely in the light you can see where he painted over the original signature."

"I'm really sorry about this. We try to make every effort to assure that our art and artists are authentic."

"I'm sure you do, Andy. Have you sold any of the other paintings he brought you?"

"Unfortunately, yes. All six of them. They were a real hit with our patrons. That's how I know he's coming in today. He was most anxious to be paid."

"Yes, I'm sure he was."

The bell jingled and John turned but it was an older woman. He looked around the gallery as Andy went to wait on the customer.

A few minutes later the door jingled again, John looked around the wall of paintings between him and the door. A young man with blonde hair came in carrying a painting. He stayed hidden while Andy greeted the man, took the canvas and lead him to his office.

"I'll be right back," Andy said to Eric. He closed the door and nodded to John. "You can use my office." He handed the painting to John.

John looked at the painting and drew a sharp breath through clenched teeth. Eric really is a low-life, he thought.

"Do you want me to call the police?"

"No, I'll handle this." John opened the office door, stepped into the room, closed the door firmly and leaned against it. Eric turned with a big smile but seeing John, the smile abruptly turned to alarm.

"Oh, sh—"

"Hello, Eric. You seem surprised to see me."

Eric swallowed hard. "I—yeah—uh. What're you doing here?"

"I came to pick up Brianna's money." John pushed away from the door and walked slowly toward Eric. Eric backed around the desk and stood behind the chair gripping the back for support. "I thought I'd save you the trouble of bringing it to her. That was what you were intending, wasn't it?"

Eric looked down, then at the door as if calculating his chances for escaping. John laughed.

"Sit down, Eric. We're going to have a little talk before I call the police."

Sweat beaded on Eric's forehead as he sat down. If John had any lingering doubts about Brianna's paintings, Eric erased them. The man was definitely guilty.

"You can't prove anything. Besides, she owed me. I supported her for nearly a year."

"On second thought," John said, grasping the front of Eric's shirt and pulling him to his feet. "I think you should stand up. Man to–," He looked down at the cowering Eric, "–man. You're lucky I'm not prone to violence but one more word out of you and that could change."

Eric opened his mouth and looked up at John defiantly. John's right hand formed a fist, his eyes narrowed.

"You're not worth it," John said, shoving him roughly into the chair. He kept his eyes on Eric as he opened the door and called Andy.

"Andy, make a check out to Mr. Hansen for the paintings and make two copies of the receipt." Andy and Eric both looked at him in surprise. "Then you and I," he said, looking at Eric, "are going to the bank so you can cash it and I'll take the cash to Brianna."

"What's to stop you from keeping the cash?" Eric said.

"Don't push me, Hansen. Do as I say and I won't call the police."

"I'd just tell them I was selling them for her."

John smiled. "I have Andy's word that you consigned the paintings in your name and there's the little detail that you painted over the original signature with your own. It doesn't look good for you." A muscle twitched in Eric's left eye and sweat again beaded his brow. "You're pathetic," John said.

"Under the circumstances, I didn't take out our usual commission," Andy said as he handed John the check.

"Thank you, Andy. I'll be sure to recommend your gallery," John said, putting the check into his breast pocket. He grasped Eric under the arm and pulled him to his feet. He kept a firm grip on his arm as he steered him out the door, down the stairs and to the bank on the corner. He didn't release him until he had the cash in his hand.

"If I were you, I'd get out of town. I gave you my word that I wouldn't call the police, but I can't speak for Brianna." John watched Eric until he rounded the corner then he turned and walked back to his car. He pulled away from the curb and headed back to his office.

* * * *

"Sandy, get Carly Ames for me, again, please," John said as he passed her desk. He went into his office, shed his jacket and wandered to the window. He smiled as he loosened his tie recalling how Brianna had called him 'stuffy.' *Had that really only been two weeks ago?* So much had changed. He had changed. He no longer felt stuffy. Thinking about Brianna made him happy. Thinking about losing her did not. He made up his mind that wasn't going to happen. He would do whatever it took to get her back.

He turned at the knock on his door. Carly stepped in. John walked back to his desk and motioned for her to sit. When she was seated, he sat down and picked up a pencil, studying it thoughtfully as if weighing his words.

"You said Brianna loved me." That was the only important thing he'd heard earlier.

Carly nodded.

"Do you think she still does, or did I ruin it?"

Carly studied his face for a few seconds before answering, "I think she'll always love you." John gave a satisfied smile. "Whether she'll forgive you is another matter." The smile faded.

"Do you think she'll talk to me?"

"I don't know. I wouldn't, but I'm not Brianna. She's a whole lot more forgiving than I am."

"Did she move into her new apartment?"

Carly hesitated before nodding, "Yes, but she's talking about going home to Ireland. If I were you, I wouldn't wait too long to find out if she'll forgive you."

CHAPTER SEVENTEEN

Brianna methodically put one foot in front of the other and reminded herself to breathe. She kicked a small stone along the sidewalk that led to her new apartment. She hated the thought of giving it up so soon but if she didn't have a job she wouldn't be able to afford it. Mrs. Whitley said not to worry but Brianna didn't want charity. The run along the lakeshore had cleared her head; unfortunately, her heart was being more difficult. Her heart, she decided, would just have to be ignored. Maybe, in time, it would heal but it would never be whole again. Part of it had been ripped away, stomped on and forever damaged. She was not going to think about that. What was over, was over. She needed to be practical—to get on with her life.

It was nearly dark when she arrived at her apartment door. A shiver ran down her spine. Her heart skipped a beat as she put the key into the lock. She instinctively looked around but saw no one... until she reached the top of the stairs.

Sitting in the over-stuffed chair was the source of her heartache.

She stopped with one hand on the newel post.

"What are you doing here?" she managed to ask despite the lump in her throat.

John stood and took a step toward her. "I want to talk to you."

"Yeah, well, I don't want to talk to you," She tightened her grip on the post since the trembling that had started in her hands now approached her knees.

John flinched at the harsh tone of Brianna's voice.

"I can understand that," he said.

"You hurt me." Brianna glared at him.

"I know and I'm sorry. Seeing him there made me angry."

"His *being* there made me angry but you wouldn't give me a chance to explain."

"You're right. I should have listened. I should have trusted you."

"It's very hard to argue with you if you keep agreeing with me." Brianna's lips thinned when John smiled. Her eyes narrowed. "How'd you get in here, anyway?"

John looked down at his feet like a small boy who'd been caught stealing cookies, "Mrs. Whitley is my aunt. She let me in after giving me a very stern lecture. It seems you have an ally." He raised his head to look at her.

"*You're* the nephew who talked her into renting this apartment?"

John nodded.

"I should have known. It was too perfect. You have to control everything," Brianna said. "I told you I could take care of myself but you didn't believe me. You don't think I'm capable of anything, do you?"

John took another step toward her. "I didn't say—"

"Don't come any closer," Brianna said. "Would you just go? I can't think straight with you here and I really need to right now." She released her death grip on the newel post and walked to the sofa, sitting on the edge, elbows on her knees, her hands clasped between them. She kept her eyes on the carpet. "Thanks to Kaitlyn, I don't have a job and now, thanks to you, I can't stay in this apartment."

"She didn't have the right to fire you so you still have a job and, just because you're angry with me doesn't mean you can't stay here. Aunt Tess is on your side."

"I've decided to go home for awhile until I can figure out how–" *I can live without you.* "What I want to do," Brianna said without looking up.

"Is there anything I could say that would change your mind?"

Brianna glanced at him and shook her head.

Reaching into his jacket pocket, John withdrew an envelope and tossed it onto the coffee table.

"Maybe this will help," he said.

"What's this?" She picked up the envelope, opened it and peered inside. "Severance pay?" She held up the cash.

"No, I told you you're not fired. I had a little talk with Eric. It seems he took it upon himself to sell your paintings and that's the proceeds."

Brianna thumbed through the cash and looked at John. "Nice try but my paintings would never bring this much. There must be over two thousand dollars here." She held it out to him. "I don't want your charity."

"It's not charity. Here's the business card for the gallery that sold them." He laid the card on the coffee table. "Check it out if you don't believe me." John walked to the stairs, stopped and turned around. "I love you."

Brianna swallowed the lump in her throat and licked a stray tear from the corner of her mouth.

251

"If you really loved me you'd trust me and you don't so there is nothing left to say."

He took a couple of steps toward her. "I'm not making excuses, but may I tell you something that might explain my reaction?"

Brianna drew a shaky breath and gave a brief nod. She stared at John's reflection in the blank television screen. He sat on the edge of the chair and picked up a pencil from the coffee table, rolling it between his palms. "Fifteen years ago I married my high school sweetheart, Michelle. We were young, too young. We were in college and had our lives planned out, everything seemed perfect. After college, I worked for a local ad agency where I met Todd Martin. We were both ambitious and anxious to advance. After a couple of years we started our own agency. We worked obsessively to build the business. Michelle complained that we never saw each other but I had to succeed, to provide all the things I thought we needed, so I continued working long hours and week-ends, never taking time off. One night, I came home from a business conference a day early, and found Michelle in bed with Todd." He paused. "Seeing you there with him–" He snapped the pencil in half.

"I'm not Michelle."

"I know that, Brianna."

She stood and turned to face him. His pained look almost melted her resolve. She took a deep breath and blinked back her tears.

"You know it here." She pointed to her head. "But not here." She moved her hand to her heart. "And, until you know it here," she patted her chest, "I can't—" She turned her back to him as tears ran freely down her cheeks. "Please go." She choked on the words and ran into the bedroom, closing the door behind her.

* * * *

Brianna awoke to the gentle chime of her doorbell. She padded barefoot to the open bedroom window. The aroma of freshly baked cinnamon rolls wafted through the opening. Mrs. Whitely stood by her front door. As much as she wanted to crawl back into bed and hide from the world, the mouth-watering scent proved too much to resist.

"I'll be right down, Mrs. Whitley." Brianna realized she still had on the clothes she wore the night before, now crumpled. She grabbed her robe from the chair, slipping it on as she descended the stairs.

"Good morning, dear." Mrs. Whitley passed the plate beneath Brianna's nose. "May I come in?"

"Yes, of course. Those smell delicious." Brianna stepped back to allow the older woman to enter and motioned for her to go up the stairs.

"Sit and I'll brew us a pot of tea." Mrs. Whitley set the plate on the table and moved to the kitchen.

"Mrs. Whitley—" Brianna began.

"Please call me Aunt Tess or just Tess, if you prefer. Mrs. Whitley seems so impersonal."

"Miss Tess, you should sit while I get the tea," Brianna said. Aunt Tess seemed too personal.

"Nonsense, dear. I imagine you had a rough night."

Brianna jerked her head up. "I— How—"

"I talked to my nephew last night, after he'd been here." Tess chuckled. "I'm guessing he had a rough night, too."

Brianna looked away wiping, a hand across her eyes. She heard the woman open the refrigerator.

"Oh, my," Tess exclaimed. "The cupboard is pretty bare."

"I'm getting ready go back to Ireland."

"John mentioned that."

"Did he ask you to talk to me?"

Tess set a tray on the table. She returned to the kitchen for plates and silverware before she answered.

"I'd be lying if I said he didn't but he didn't tell me what to say." She buttered a roll, put it on a plate and pushed it toward Brianna.

"I'm surprised he didn't. He likes to control everything." Brianna poured the tea, adding cream and sugar to hers.

Tess smiled. "Let me tell you a little about John. He's a very capable and responsible man." Brianna nodded. That much she knew. "Even as a little boy he wasn't really a child. He was very caring, always bringing home stray dogs, cats or injured birds to fix. You name it, he wanted to fix it."

"Is that what I am, a stray he wants to fix?"

"Not you, dear, just your situation. If it's within his power to help, to make someone's life better, he will. His mother, bless her heart, was a professor of medieval poetry. She was brilliant in her field but not bothered with mundane tasks. John's father, my brother, took care of her, making sure she ate and did all the things one needs to do in daily life. John grew up thinking all women need to be taken care of."

"I don't need taking care of. I've been bossed around all my life. I don't want anyone controlling me."

"Of course you don't. But you need to realize the difference between controlling and caring. John cares. He cares very much. He just needs to learn not everything needs fixing."

Brianna stirred her tea. "I don't think my heart can take any more grief." She caught a tear before it rolled down her cheek.

Tess put her hand on Brianna's arm. "I understand, dear. You go on home to your family. Everything will look clearer there. Just remember that he really does love you."

Brianna stood to clear the dishes, retreating to the kitchen. Tess followed and gave her a hug which was nearly Brianna's undoing. Thankfully, the woman left before tears consumed her again.

Crossing the living room, she saw the envelope containing the cash John had left on the coffee table. She picked it up. *Why wait?*

* * * *

John sat at his desk rubbing his temples. He needed a plan to keep Brianna from leaving. No, he needed a plan to make her want to stay.

His cell rang. It was his aunt.

"I'm alright. Or, I will be. Someday. Maybe." He stood and paced to the window. He stared, unseeing at the lake below.

"She did what? When?" John nearly yelled.

He listened to Aunt Tess a second.

"I'll think of something. Thanks, Aunt Tess."

He straightened, turned and grabbed his jacket from the back of the chair.

"Sandy, I'm leaving for the day," He said to his surprised secretary as he passed her desk.

* * * *

Brianna boarded the plane, grateful she was able to get a window seat near the back. She stared at the raindrops trickling down the window. The darkness enveloped her and she had to fight to keep the tears at bay.

As the flight attendant gave the pre-flight instructions, Brianna checked her seatbelt. The plane rolled back then proceeded to the runway. Shortly after the captain announced they had reached their cruising altitude, the flight attendant approached her.

"Miss Ryan, you've been selected for an upgrade to first class."

"I'm sure there's been a mistake." Brianna said.

"No, miss. There are empty seats in front. It's standard policy to offer an upgrade."

" I'm fine here, really. Perhaps someone else would appreciate it."

The attendant persisted. *I may as well wallow in comfort.* Brianna relented and followed her up the aisle to the first class cabin. The dimly lit space was empty, except for an older couple in the front and a man in the back reading a newspaper. She took a window seat near the middle. The attendant handed her a pillow and blanket before returning to the galley.

A few minutes later, she returned carrying a tray with a glass of Champagne and a rose. Brianna shook her head.

"It's complimentary, miss." The young woman said as she set it on her tray-table. "We'll be serving dinner shortly."

The last thing Brianna wanted was Champagne or food. She picked up the rose. It was an Irish Rose. She turned it over in her hands, tears forming on her lashes. She dabbed the corner of her eyes with the linen napkin and picked up the flute, bringing it to her lips.

She signaled the attendant. "There's something in the bottom of the glass."

"Why, yes, there is." She smiled and looked toward the back row as a newspaper was noisily folded. When the attendant retreated to the galley, a man slid into the seat beside Brianna.

"It's an emerald ring. It was my grandmother's."

Brianna couldn't speak through the lump in her throat. Her heart beat was surely visible. She stared open mouthed as John fished the ring from the bottom of the flute.

"I heard from a very reliable source that you love me." John dried the ring with a napkin.

Brianna gave a slight nod, her hand covering her mouth as tears filled her eyes.

"I know I love you and I know I don't want to live without you. I know it here." He touched his forehead. "And, I know it here." He spread his hand over his heart. "Will you marry me?" He brought her left hand to his lips and waited for her answer.

Brianna nodded. Tears spilled down her cheeks.

John slipped the ring on her finger. He pulled her onto his lap. Brianna threw her arms around his neck and met his lips with a forever kind of kiss.

ABOUT THE AUTHOR

Sarah Purcell lives in El Paso, Texas with her husband, Jim, their dog, Phoebe and cat named Boo.

An avid reader her entire life, she turned to writing after her nest was empty. She spends much of her free time dreaming up new happily-ever-after stories.

Coming in 2016

Love Is a Game